Stuart is a professor emeritus of lifelong learning. He retired from full-time work at the University in 2010. Since then, he has continued to write, publish, and present in his academic field of expertise. He also has begun writing fiction – and especially fiction fantasy for young children. *The Land of Faerie* is the latest in a series known as *The Molly Adventures*. Stuart and his wife Dilys share their time between their home near York in the UK, and another in SE Spain. Along with writing, he loves to watch sports on TV and occasionally loves playing golf.

The
Land
of
Faerie

Stuart C. Billingham

AUSTIN MACAULEY PUBLISHERS™
LONDON • CAMBRIDGE • NEW YORK • SHARJAH

A CIP catalogue record for this title is available from the British Library.

ISBN 9781398499966 (Paperback)
ISBN 9781398499973 (ePub e-book)

www.austinmacauley.com

First Published 2023
Austin Macauley Publishers Ltd®
1 Canada Square
Canary Wharf
London
E14 5AA

This work is dedicated to my wife, Dilys, who supports me in so many ways, all of which help me to believe in myself and to find the time and space to write.

Chapter One

Unicorn was sleeping in the shade of a large oak tree near the middle of the forest when he was woken by some strange sounds not too far away. Unicorn was not best pleased.

He had been awake for much of the previous night, involved in the dreams of a young boy named Tom. Tom was a highly active young boy when he was awake, and his dreams were equally active and busy. That meant Unicorn had been busy all night too. It was not until Tom finally awoke from his dreams, in the morning, that Unicorn had a chance for some sleep.

As a unicorn, he was used to being awake through the night being in the dreams of people – mostly younger ones – who imagined unicorns during their sleep. However, Tom's dreams were particularly active and busy. Tom wanted Unicorn to be doing all sorts of things during them. Sometimes he was riding across fields with Tom on his back; another time it would be through woodland, and not just with Tom on his back but also some of his friends, including his friend Molly. At other times Tom would be trying to skewer apples onto Unicorn's horn and sometimes he wanted Unicorn to speak to him and others in his dreams. And so, it went on.

Most nights, within other folks' dreams, things were much quieter. More often than not, Unicorn was simply a background part of the dream and not doing very much at all. Maybe he would meander through his wood, eating grass and cleaning his horn on the bark of trees. He had several magical powers but almost no one knew about these, as they never occurred in the dreams.

So, after this particular night within Tom's dreams, Unicorn was especially tired. He had not been long asleep when the sounds gradually got nearer and nearer to where he had settled for some much-needed rest.

"Goodness me. What in the name of a pixie's ears is going on?" he said to himself, as he stretched, yawned a very wide and exceptionally long yawn, and then slowly began to stand-up. He looked in the direction of the noise. "Ah. Elves."

As is usually the case when elves move around together, this group was surrounded by a bright white light, and they were making a sweet, rhythmical sound which is what had woken him. Unicorn could see some things through the light. There were seven elves. Six of them, three on each side, surrounding another one as they progressed through the wood. As they came ever closer, it was easier for Unicorn to see the group, but he had

to be careful. The louder the beautifully sweet sound became, the more hypnotic it became too. Unicorn was fully aware of this and though he could lessen and soften the sound he heard using his magical powers, he could not stop hearing it altogether. The elves' magic, especially when they were together like this, was too powerful for that. Unicorn concentrated hard on the 'chief elf' walking majestically in the middle of the group.

He or she – he couldn't tell from this distance, but it didn't matter to him anyway – was very majestic. They were beautiful, with an 'other-worldly' appearance. Tall, thin and elegant. Some would have called them 'angels' but they are different, especially in terms of what they can and can't do. Suddenly, the group came to a stop and the sweet sound from before also stopped. Gradually, the white light which had surrounded the elven group faded and became a type of haze, making it easier to see all the elves but still not completely clearly. Suddenly, Unicorn heard a voice which he guessed was coming from the 'chief elf' though from this distance, and with the surrounding haze, he couldn't see their lips moving.

"Sir Unicorn. It seems we have broken your much-needed sleep. I am sorry about that. I do apologise for it." At that, the elves bowed and then sank on to their knees with head lowered. They didn't move.

"It is my honour to welcome you to this part of The Great Wood, though I am afraid I do not know your name to address you properly," said Unicorn. He was not fazed by being addressed as 'Sir Unicorn', as this was how all elves addressed unicorns. It was a sign of respect for their great age and beauty, as well as their quite significant magical powers.

"I am Carolina. Queen Carolina of the Southern wood." And with that, the elf stood up.

Even through the haze surrounding the elven group, it was clear now that Queen Carolina was wonderfully beautiful. A pale, almost translucent, skin with very dark, large round eyes; her long, dark, blonde hair was tied up onto the top and back of her head – which was unusual for elven Queens –sitting beneath a plain silver and gold crown and wearing a shimmering silver-white gown bedecked with various jewels.

"So, Queen Carolina, what, may I ask, brings you to this part of the Wood. You are a long way from your usual home many leagues from here." The Queen smiled – a beautifully warm and gentle smile.

"Thank you for being so thoughtful Sir Unicorn. I have not heard the expression 'leagues' for a long time. I have become used to more modern terms of measurement – such as miles or metres – having listened to humans use such words."

Unicorn smiled and bowed his head in respect to the elven Queen.

"Well, I think this part of the wood is more-or-less 30 kilometres from your domain. Am I right perhaps?

"Yes, almost," said the Queen, "But no matter. We are now here together, and I think our paths have crossed because fate wished that it should be so."

Unicorn thought about this for some time. *Why would fate wish that he and the elf Queen meet together? Even more importantly, even if fate did wish it then why here at this spot, and why now?*

Chapter Two

Even as Unicorn mused to himself as to why it seemed so important that he and elven Queen Carolina should meet at this time, and in that place in the Great Wood, part of the answer began to appear in front of his eyes. They came from the north, the east and the west.

Just as when Queen Carolina had arrived, there were seven elves in each group. Six of them, three on each side, surrounded another one as they progressed through the Wood from all corners of the compass, except of course the south.

As with Queen Carolina's group, each of the others was surrounded by a bright white light which seemed to give out a beautifully sweet sound. Strangely, as Unicorn thought even then, the sound of each group was different and yet they all blended to make a quite remarkable, and harmonious sound which was almost perfect. As he realised later, it was, of course, missing the sound of the elven Queen Carolina of the Southern Wood which would have made it complete and perfect.

As each group arrived, they stationed themselves at the three points of the compass around where Queen Carolina stood with Unicorn. Each group stood silently and still, with their bright white lights reduced to a calming haze, and a corresponding softening of the beautiful sound they made. Then, Queen Carolina spoke. It was not a language Unicorn could understand easily, but in our language, she said;

"Welcome my friends and guardians of The Great Wood. It is a long time since we have all been together. We meet here at this time and in this place because we must do so." At this point there were some noises – a little like grumbling – from the northern group, but they soon subsided, and the Queen continued.

"We have set-out over many years to ensure that those called humans do not forget who we are. That they do not think we only exist in the stories they read as young children on the dry pages of their books. We have a duty to do what we can to make sure all humans believe in our world, and experience all the wonderful things we can bring to their imaginations, emotions and feelings." At this point there were more sounds from the groups, but this time it somehow sounded more positive, more affirming. Queen Carolina sensed that too and smiled.

"So, now I ask the Princesses and Prince to share with us – for the benefit of Sir Unicorn here near me – your names and where you are from."

"I am Prince Charlelot, Prince of the North Wood. I bid you a very good day Sir Unicorn and I hope it will prove to be good for all of us." Unicorn bowed his head gracefully in the direction of the Prince, who was still stood in the middle of his group.

"And I am Princess Esmeralda, Queen over all in the Eastern Wood. I too bid you well, Sir Unicorn." Unicorn once again bowed his head.

"And last but certainly not least, I am Princess Josephina, Queen of the Western Wood. It is good to see you again Sir Unicorn. It has been a long, long time." Unicorn bowed his head, saying;

"Yes, it has my Lady Princess. Those were dark and difficult times which I hope will never return to The Great Wood."

Just as Unicorn finished what he was saying and raised his head, an elf not from any of the groups, ran into the area where they were all gathered. It stopped well away from any of the groups, bowed to the Prince, to each of the Princesses and to Queen Carolina. He then stood quite still. He was dressed mainly in gold-coloured material which was not a colour associated with any of the four woods which made up The Great Wood. Queen Carolina was the first to speak, and in a very authoritarian and not at all friendly manner.

"And to whom am I speaking when I ask what you want here with us?" The elf turned to face the Queen, bowed again, and then said, "My name is Goodkind, my Lady Queen."

"And from where do you come to us today?"

"I come from the White Wood not far from The Great Wood on its eastern side."

Princess Esmeralda now emerged from within her group. She was, like Queen Carolina, a most beautiful elf. Tall, slim, dressed in shades of blue and with long blonde hair which reached down her back to her waist. Her crown was, like Queen Carolina's, very simple and made of gold and silver.

"And what can you tell us of the White Wood, my sister?" said Queen Carolina looking straight at Esmeralda and to no one else.

"We know the White Wood well, as you would imagine. Our lives near to each other have not always been friendly. We and they remember the darkest days of what we call 'The Wars'. There was much destruction, and many elves did not survive."

Esmeralda dropped her head almost to her chest and Unicorn could see tears rolling down her cheeks. He looked across and Goodkind's head was lowered too. He could not see if there were any tears. After a short pause, Princess Esmeralda slowly lifted her head and continued.

"However, we have spent many years resolving the issues between us; repairing the destruction; and creating friendships so that there will be no repeat of those dark days. Today, we have good relations with The White Wood and, I believe, they have with us."

Everyone looked across at Goodkind. He did not hesitate in his answer.

"The Lady Princess Esmeralda is correct and we in The White Wood are grateful for our friendship. We wish above all else that it will last for many centuries and, hopefully, for ever."

"So, what brings you to us today Elf Goodkind?"

"The message I bring is from my Lord Oakenleaf." At this, he reached into the small bag hanging from his side and took out an even smaller piece of cloth. He unfolded it and read out loud so everyone could hear.

"Our gateways to humans, which we know you value so highly as do we, are no longer reliable. I fear that very soon we will have no gateways."

Unicorn could sense tension run through the assembled elves from across The Great Wood at this news. At this moment, Princess Josephina stepped from within her group. Like Carolina and Esmeralda, she was stunningly beautiful. Slim and tall with long blonde hair she wore a gown of many shades of red, lilac and purple. Her crown was also very simple in design, and of gold and silver like theirs.

"Like all of my brothers and sisters gathered here I am sure, I do not welcome this news. But how do we know it is true? What evidence can Elf Goodkind give us?"

Lord Oakenleaf had clearly known this question would be asked, because he had prepared his messenger Goodkind with a way of showing the evidence they had."

"I thank my Lady Princess for this question. If it is agreed, I can try to show you all the evidence we have for this."

Unicorn could see no reason to reject this offer, but he knew that elves, especially those of noble birth and in positions of responsibility, could be very suspicious creatures. Queen Carolina looked at the assembled groups and then asked Goodkind one obvious and one curious question.

"So, Elf Goodkind, how will you show us this evidence? Will it involve any special powers you may have?"

Everyone turned to look at Goodkind. Unicorn looked at him hard. His own 'special powers' could be used to determine when creatures were telling the truth or were evading it. He found it impossible to penetrate Goodkind's mind which he found unusual and, for that reason, worrying. Goodkind didn't look at Unicorn but fixed his gaze on Queen Carolina.

"I have my Lord's Orb and his permission to use it if necessary." His tone was assertive and quite different to how he had spoken, up to this point. Queen Carolina looked towards Princess Esmeralda but this time she did not speak to her using her tongue but instead using her mind.

"What do you know of this Orb, my sister?"

"We know little about it. It is kept by the Lord Oakenleaf and we believe it enables him to see into the past and into the future."

"An interesting device indeed. Do we trust the Messenger and this 'Orb'?"

"I think we have little choice Carolina. I am sure that with our number here, we can deal with the Messenger if necessary and stop any adverse things which may come from the Orb".

This conversation took but just a second or two, so no one knew it had even happened. Carolina then said out loud, "If you are content Esmeralda, then we will proceed." Esmeralda nodded.

"Go ahead Elf Goodkind. Show us your evidence."

perfect. As he realised later, it was, of course, missing the sound of the elven Queen Carolina of the Southern Wood which would have made it complete and perfect.

As each group arrived, they stationed themselves at the three points of the compass around where Queen Carolina stood with Unicorn. Each group stood silently and still, with their bright white lights reduced to a calming haze, and a corresponding softening of the beautiful sound they made. Then, Queen Carolina spoke. It was not a language Unicorn could understand easily, but in our language, she said;

"Welcome my friends and guardians of The Great Wood. It is a long time since we have all been together. We meet here at this time and in this place because we must do so." At this point there were some noises – a little like grumbling – from the northern group, but they soon subsided, and the Queen continued.

Chapter Three

"Molly. Molleee? MOLLEEEE?"

It was the usual evening call by her Dad. He guessed, or more accurately knew, where he would find his daughter at this time of the evening just before supper at seven o'clock, but he just had to call anyway. So, when he got no response, he went from the dining room, down the long hallway, off to the left through his study, and into the "sun-room". Many would have called it a conservatory, but everyone agreed it was too small for that. Nevertheless, it was made mainly of glass, received lots of sun, and gave a great view of the rear garden.

As usual, he found Molly sat in her favourite armchair which, being designed for adults to use, seemed to cuddle her like a huge teddy bear might do with his arms gently wrapped around her. She was looking out into the garden and directly at the glass lantern which hung from one of the hooks on the bird feeder, just to the left in a small flower bed.

For a while her dad stood looking at her, wondering what it was she saw in this light most evenings. He had asked her this question many times but all she would say was, "Just interesting stuff, Dad."

He had stared at the light himself on many evenings but what he saw was...well...a light, giving out a pale white glow across the garden. It was just that, a light. Sometimes, there were birds flying around the garden but none of them seemed interested in the lantern.

The lantern was made of fashioned or "wobbly" glass as Molly called it, with stainless steel rings at the top and bottom. It was about twenty centimetres high and ten centimetres in diameter. On what you might call the roof of the lantern were some small solar panels which recharged its batteries each day, ready for the lightshow the following evening.

"C'mon Molly. Time for supper. Your friends in the light will still be there I am sure after you have finished." Molly turned and stared at her dad.

"How do you know my friends are there, Dad? How do you know?"

Molly's dad was taken by surprise at the sharpness in the way Molly asked him the questions. He decided 'discretion was the better part of valour' as the old saying goes, or in modern speech that he should 'back-off'.

"Well, I don't know anything about it, Molly. I am just assuming..." His voice trailed off.

"Anyway, whatever the case, its time you came for supper. C'mon now. Let's go." At that, he turned and moved toward the door, then looked back at Molly who was still staring at him. He motioned for her to follow him. Suddenly, she stopped staring at him, took one further glance back at the lantern and then followed her dad out of the door, along the hallway and joined her Mum in the dining room.

"Late as usual young lady, I see."

Molly looked sheepishly down at her shoes and shuffled slightly. She then took her seat at the table and began to tuck into her lovely meal.

Molly's mum and dad looked at each other across the table and shrugged their shoulders. "We'll have to find out what is going on with that lantern," Molly's mum whispered to her husband.

Chapter Four

It had seemed a long time but in fact it was only a couple of days, and Molly couldn't resist the urge anymore to ask her dad why the lantern didn't seem to be working properly. In truth, it was that it was hit-and-miss. Some evenings it worked fine and shone brightly. At other times, the light was very dull and might even go off altogether. So, one evening when the light was dull and even flickering occasionally, she plucked-up the courage to ask what was happening whilst she and her Mum and Dad were having supper.

"Dad?"

"Yes Molly. What is it?"

"Well, have you noticed how some nights the lantern is shining brightly and then other nights, like tonight, it is very dull?"

"To be honest, I haven't noticed that, Molly. I don't look at the lantern that often and certainly not every night the way you do." When Molly had her head down putting food onto her fork, her Mum gave her dad a knowing wink. Perhaps this was their chance to find out what it was that intrigued their young and inquisitive daughter about the lantern.

"I suspect it might be the solar panels, or the

batteries which they charge using the light from the sun, which are on the blink. I'll have to take it apart and see if new batteries will solve the problem. That's a lot easier than replacing the solar panels unless we have to."

"Well, how long will it take to change the batteries?"

"It shouldn't take very long at all but first I'll have to take out the ones in it now and see if I have any new ones of the right size."

"And if you haven't got any? Will the light be off very long?"

"Goodness me young lady it's question, question, question with you about this blinking lantern," interrupted her Mum. "What would it matter if it were off for several days before your dad could fix it? You might be on holidays but bear in mind he is at work every day as you well know."

"Several days!!!" Molly exclaimed. "It wouldn't be that long, would it Dad?"

"Well, Molly, it could be. It depends on what I need to do, and need to buy, to fix it. Anyway, why would it matter so much?" Both her mum and dad stopped eating and waited expectantly for the answer.

"Well, you see. I mean...well, I don't suppose it would matter all that much, except..." Her voice trailed off, and she sat staring at her plate.

"C'mon Molly. Whatever it is, you can share it with your mum and I. We are just interested."

Molly mumbled a few words but still sat staring at her plate.

"We didn't hear any of that Molly. Now, c'mon. What are you worried about?"

There was a fairly long silence, during which all that could be heard was the ticking of the grandfather clock standing regally in the dining room corner near to the sunroom doors. Suddenly, Molly blurted it out.

"I'm sorry Dad. I'm sorry Mum. But I will tell you everything once the light is working properly again, and hopefully as soon as is possible. I promise I will."

"What a little negotiator we have raised, Mr Stevens," said Molly's Mum smiling and starting to chuckle. "I think she follows in her grandfather Steven's footsteps."

"Why do you say that, Mum? What does Grandpa Peter have to do with it?"

"Well, Molly, his job before he retired was to try and get people who disagreed about important things in their lives to come to an agreement about them. He was what was called a 'negotiator'. One of the ways he used to do this was to say, "Well Mr A, if you do X then I think Miss B will do Z, which is what you want and would be good for all of us."

Molly sat back in her chair and thought about what her mum had said. She eventually realised she was right. She was agreeing to tell them what they wanted to know if her dad repaired the light as quickly as possible.

"So, I think I get it. Dad is Mr A and if he repairs the light as fast as he can, what you called 'X', then I, who am Miss B in your story, will tell you about the light and stuff, which is what you called 'Z'. Is that right, Mum?"

"Got it in one Miss B. Now, it's time for some dessert."

Chapter Five

Two days later was Saturday and Molly's dad now had time to try and find out what might be wrong with the lantern.

As he retrieved it from where it hung in the garden and took it into his tool shed – or what his wife and their friends called his 'man cave' – he wondered if the problem was simply that it was old and had started to leak, allowing water into the battery compartment. As he carried it to his shed, he noticed there was some water inside, but it was very little.

In the house, Molly was gulping down her breakfast cereal and fruit, frequently looking out of the kitchen window towards the tool shed.

"Look Molly," said her Mum, as she finished washing-up some of the breakfast dishes. "Your dad isn't going to disappear suddenly with the lantern. You can go and join him in the cave once you have finished your breakfast and washed up your dishes. OK?"

"OK Mum."

Meanwhile in the tool shed, Molly's dad had removed the batteries and had checked whether he had any new re-chargeable ones which would fit into the lantern. He didn't. So, his first job was to drive to his nearest DIY store to buy some.

It wasn't too far away – maybe 15 minutes or so to get there – but he decided it was well worth trying to remove the solar panels first and take them with him to see if the store had any which would replace them.

Molly met her dad part way between the shed and the house.

"What's happening Dad? What's happening?"

"I'm off to the DIY store, Molly. Do you want to come? It's best to get new batteries and new solar panels if I can."

About an hour later they returned home. As Molly got out of the car, it was clear to her mum waiting to let them in at the front door, that Molly was not happy at all. It was raining hard, and Molly and her dad ran quickly into the house.

"Phew. A day just for ducks to be out and about," said Molly's mum, trying as best she could to lighten the mood of the returning pair. When Molly continued to look glum, her Mum had no choice but to ask, "So, what's the news?"

"Well, we found a really great assistant in the shop who knew all sorts of things about such batteries and also the solar panels. She is a student at the university studying electro-physics and chemistry," said Molly's dad.

"And?"

"So, she tested the batteries, and they were not

working properly anymore, so I've bought a new set. To my surprise, she was also able to test the solar panels and they are working fine. So, I'll change the batteries now and after a day or perhaps two once they have had time to fully charge themselves through the solar panels, the lantern should be working fine." He then went out of the kitchen to the small bathroom along the hallway, to wash his hands.

"So, why such a glum face, Molly?"

Molly had been drying her hair and her face on a hand towel in the kitchen. She looked at her mum.

"I don't know Mum. It seems such good news and Mandy at the shop was brilliant. I just have all my fingers and my toes crossed that once Dad has changed the batteries the lantern will be working just as it did."

"But you don't sound hopeful, Molly. Why is that?" There was a silence and Molly looked around and then down at her feet, as if hoping for something else to talk about. Her dad heard the end of the conversation as he walked back into the kitchen.

"Why don't we wait until we see how the new batteries change things, eh Molly? I'll change them after some lunch. I'm starving."

Molly looked up at him and smiled.

"OK Dad." She looked across and smiled at her Mum.

"I'm hungry too now that I think of it. What's for lunch?"

It was Molly's favourite lunch, at least on a warm day – cheese, a little cooked ham, some mixed salad, potatoes, and lots of mayonnaise. Afterwards, she knew she couldn't explore the lantern. She would have to wait for her dad to fit the new batteries, and then wait some more to see if they made the necessary difference and the lantern started to work again. So, she went to her bedroom and played with some of her favourite toys. After about an hour, with a full stomach and feeling satisfied, she began to doze. It was not long before she fell into a deep and comfortable sleep, curled-up on top of her bed.

Chapter Six

The elves attendant on Prince Charlelot of the Northern Wood were not happy with how things were progressing at this "gathering". They had long believed they should be the dominant force in the Great Wood and their Prince should be its leader. Instead, it seemed that Princess Carolina always dominated any coming-together of those from the different areas of the wood. The same was happening again this time.

However, they were mainly suspicious of – and hostile toward – any idea which seemed to want to involve humans in their lives. Why would the folk of Faerie – a world inhabited by themselves, pixies, and other wonderful creatures such as Unicorns – want to invite humans into their world? It made no sense. All that they had read or heard about humans showed their destructive and war-like tendencies. The Land of Faerie was about living together peacefully and cooperatively. Yes, there were disagreements, but these passed in a fleeting second to be replaced by a simple solution which everyone could – and did – accept.

The Northern Wood had campaigned for many hundreds of years – in human terms – to abandon the pursuit of human contact. Their idea was to let humans discover the world of Faerie through their children's stories and then let them enter it through their dreams if they wanted to know more. The strategy to engage humans in other ways was a big mistake and the world of Faerie would suffer through it.

The only problem was that Prince Charlelot was not a strong Prince. He liked the quiet and enjoyable life and always tended to agree with the Princesses and Queen so that he could avoid any conflict. Many of those who lived in Northern Wood took the view that little did their good Prince realise that actively bringing humans into his world would be likely to disturb his quiet and peaceful life by increasing disagreements within it.

As they all waited to find out what this gathering was about, and for Goodkind to reveal the evidence he had said was the main reason for him being there, the attendant elves of the Northern Wood "spoke" with the attendant elves from the other woods. They "spoke" not with words which anyone could hear, but from 'mind to mind', as all elves can do if they wish.

"So, what is this all about?"

"We have no idea really, but Princess Josephina is suspicious of why we have an elf from the White Wood leading things."

"Our Princess Esmeralda seems at peace with what is going on, and we trust her in everything. She led us through the wars, and we were safe. She has our full trust."

"But the wars did not involve humans and none of us except you from the Eastern Wood have any knowledge of those in the White Wood."

"This is true, but at least we should see what evidence Goodkind has, and which has bought us all here today it seems."

"We agree with this but reserve our right to speak out against any plans to further engage with humans," said the elves from Northern Wood.

All the elves who had been party to this conversation, nodded at each other. And so, it was agreed. Once again, this 'mind-to-mind' conversation took just a few seconds. Once they had finished, they turned to look at Goodkind to see what he would do. Unicorn, Prince Charlelot, the two Princesses and Queen Carolina were looking at him too.

"Can you all see me clearly?" he said. Everyone nodded. At this moment, he took from under his cloak a small glass orb and held it in two hands out in front of him. He then spoke in the formal high-elvish tongue and said, in our language;

"Orb of Great Lord Oakenleaf, hear me. I am Goodkind, servant to the Great Lord." There was a pause and then the orb began to glow with a pinkish-white flame. "It is time to show our many friends gathered here the moving pictures of the gateways with humans. Project them in front of me. Do it now."

At the command, the orb began to glow brighter and to make a high-pitched whistling sound. This went on for a few seconds. Then the whistling sound stopped and moving pictures – similar to films as we know them – began to display in front of Goodkind and the gathered elves.

At first, it was difficult for anyone to see what the pictures were until they had tuned-in to seeing 'films'. Then they began to realise that the pictures were of many different objects, seemingly in many different places. What they were watching were different lights: some not showing any sign of life at all; some shining quite brightly; others shining with just a dull light and some flickering haphazardly. The films went on for some time and then suddenly stopped. The orb's light returned to how it had been before the projection of the 'films'.

The assembled elves stood in silence, somewhat in awe of what they had just seen. Unicorn stood motionless, wondering what the elves would make of the 'moving pictures'. It was Queen Carolina who broke the silence.

"This was truly remarkable. Elf Goodkind and I thank you; but of course, above all, we must thank your master, Lord Oakenleaf, for enabling us to see these moving pictures." The assembled elves all applauded softly – a sign, among elves, of their respect and their appreciation of the one they are applauding. Goodkind bowed slowly to the assembly.

"So, elves of The Great Wood. What do we think about what we have seen through the generosity of Lord Oakenleaf?" Again, there was silence.

Then, Prince Charlelot said;

"I think it would be wise if we consulted with our attendant elves before we offer any opinion. They may or may not be representative of all the elves who live in our parts of The Wood, but we should in any case hear their thoughts."

Queen Carolina looked towards Esmeralda and Josephina, and then to Unicorn. They each nodded.

"So be it. I suggest we will need no more than a few minutes to hear from each of our attendees." The Prince and the Princesses nodded their agreement. And so began multiple conversations, mostly mind-to-mind, within each of the groups. After about 15 seconds, Queen Carolina asked for each group to share their thoughts.

"We will start with Northern Wood. Prince Charlelot?"

"Well, we are not sure what we have seen. Yes, we know that the gateways are always through devices which use light. Yes, it seems clear that many of these gateways are not working properly. What we do not know is why that might be. Maybe they will start to work fully again. We just do not know."

"And Princess Jospehina from Western Wood?"

"It may seem strange, but we reached the same conclusion as our friends from Northern Wood."

"And so did we," said Princess Esmeralda. At that moment, they all looked to Queen Carolina. Would Southern Wood agree with everyone else?

"And we agree too, but we also said that we need to find out whether there is anything which the gateways have in common – other than being 'Gateways to the Land of Faerie' – which might be causing these problems." All the elves from the four corners of The Great Wood nodded, as did Goodkind. Then, Queen Carolina turned to Unicorn.

"And you Sir Unicorn, what can your wisdom tell us?" Unicorn stood quietly and thought for some time before he replied.

"Thank you, Queen Carolina. I think the wisdom of elves is, as always, quite remarkable. From what I saw, I agree especially with your view that we should try to discover what, if anything, all these gateways have in common which might explain the situation. My only reservation is, I do not know how we might do that."

All the elves started to look at each other with questioning expressions and gestures. How would they do that?

Chapter Seven

Time in the Land of Faerie does not pass in the same way as it does for us humans in our lives. Nevertheless, the Gathering of elves of The Great Wood had lasted a long time, even by their standards. Unicorn began to sense that night-time was falling in the land of humans, and soon he might be called into their dreams.

"My Queen Carolina," he said, bowing his head as he always did when addressing elven Princes, Princesses and Queens. The Queen looked up.

"Yes, Sir Unicorn? You sound concerned."

"I fear, my Queen, that I may soon be called into the dreams of young humans. It is close to their night-time, and I can feel the pull of their dreams upon me."

"Then you must leave us Sir Unicorn. Your work in the dreams of young humans – or any humans – is very important. It may be that we are all still here when you are done. As you know, our time moves differently to that of humans. But we wish you well. Return to us safely when you can."

"Thank you, my Queen." And at that Unicorn began to disappear. At first his outline became vague and then he started to become 'ghost-like'. Slowly, he faded altogether and then...he was gone.

It was just a few seconds before Unicorn was in a very different part of the wood. He was not sure, but he thought he might be near the Southern Wood. Even though he was in the dream-world of one or more humans who he couldn't see at present, and not in the real Great Wood where he had been with the elves, there was plenty of lush grass growing beneath the trees and he realised that after all the work with The Gathering he was now quite hungry. He started grazing.

After much too short a time – well, as far as Unicorn was concerned, that is – he saw a young boy running towards him. He hoped this was not Tom or one of his friends. Those night times were very energetic, and a quiet night would suit him well this night. As it happened it didn't look like Tom, and Unicorn breathed a sigh of relief.

The boy stopped abruptly as soon as he saw Unicorn. He stood, staring at Unicorn, about 20 metres away. Unicorn resumed his grazing. After all, it was for the boy to approach him – to be curious and inquisitive, which are wonderful traits that Unicorns try to develop in those humans they meet in their dreams.

After a short time, the boy began to take small and hesitant steps forward. Then suddenly, and from nowhere, appeared two other people. A woman dressed in a long grey gown, and a man dressed in a suit which looked like ones you might see on someone from the nineteenth century or Victorian times. When he saw them, the boy turned and started to run towards them. He was shouting to them. It sounded like, "Grandma! Grandpa! Come and see the funny horse. Let's go for a ride, shall we? Can we?" The two people stood still and didn't answer. Then, as fast as they had appeared, they disappeared. The boy sat down in the grass and began crying. A large dog now appeared and came to the boy. It sat down beside him and began to lick his arm. The boy stopped crying and began to smile, putting both his arms around the dog's neck. After a few seconds, he started stroking it along its back. Unicorn watched all these things and didn't think them at all strange. This was often what it was like inside human dreams – random events seemingly unconnected. Then, even as the boy and the dog sat together a young girl appeared in the near distance and came running towards them. She was shouting something to the boy. Unicorn listened carefully and as she came closer, he heard what she was saying, "Tom! Tom! It still won't work. It doesn't work. What am I going to do? Can you help me, Tom?" The boy looked up and Unicorn could see that the boy was indeed Tom, though he hadn't been before. The boy, now Tom, shook his head, and in a flash he and the dog, and then the girl, were gone. It was Molly and, he knew from other dreams of hers, that Tom was her best friend.

'These are rare happenings even for dreams,' Unicorn said to himself, 'I haven't been in a dream like this one for a very long time'. However, it wasn't too long before it became even stranger. A lot of people – older ones, young ones, and many in between, began to appear in the Wood. The first thing he noticed was that they were all wearing different types and styles of clothing. After being in so many human's dreams, Unicorn could recognise several of the different clothes.

Some were wearing clothes typical of Europeans, Americans, or those from Australasia and South America. Others were wearing clothing of people from the Asian sub-continent – India, Pakistan and elsewhere. Yet others, wore clothes that were traditional in China or Mongolia. Some, mainly women, wore traditional African dress. However, there were others whose dress style Unicorn did not recognise.

The other thing he noticed quickly was that they were all talking about something not working, just like the girl shouting to Tom, and what they could do about it. Then, a few of these people spotted Unicorn and began to say, pointing towards him, "Ah! He will know what we can do. He must know."

Unicorn was very confused. *'How could all these people be part of the same dream. Is it possible that they all know each other and are dreaming about each other at the same time?'* he said to himself. *'They seem to be from so many different countries in the human world. How could they know each other.'* He had never experienced anything like this. At that, they started to move, all together, toward him. Unicorn decided to 'stand his ground'. After all, these were not real 'flesh-and-blood' people. What harm could they do? And in any event, he wanted to know what was going on in the lives of these people to create this weirdest of weird dreams. He started by asking the first of the group who approached him.

"And what do you want kind, sir?"

"I suppose we each want many things Mr Unicorn but mainly, our contact with our Faerie friends is now very 'hit-and-miss'. Sometimes, we can see them easily and clearly, sometimes our gateways don't work at all. We do not know what the problem is with the gateways through which we 'meet' and speak with them. We think about this much of the time. Can you help us?"

Unicorn had not expected this. He knew, of course, that there was a problem with the gateways. One thing he hadn't known was just how much contact with those from The Land of Faerie meant to so many humans.

"I am sorry my friends, but I do not have a solution to your problem. I do know that..." but before he could finish, the people began to disappear one by one at lightning speed, and even more quickly than they had appeared.

Chapter Eight

Molly had twice been part of this 'weirdest of weird' dreams as Unicorn thought of it – once with her friend Tom and then with the folks from different parts of the human world. In that latter part of the dream, she was about to come forward to talk with Unicorn and tell him, and everyone else, what she thought the problem with the gateways could be – such as wonky solar panels and even old batteries – when everyone began to disappear. Before she could get any words out of her mouth, she had left the dream too.

When she woke up, she was sweating across her forehead, and she felt very agitated. She lay on top of her bed, turning onto her side to look out of the window. She had no idea how long she had been asleep, but it was very dull and cloudy outside and it seemed to be slowly getting darker and darker. By now, she was feeling less anxious and wanted to run downstairs and tell her mum about the dream and of all the other people who had lost touch with their friends from Faerie. Then, as she swung her legs out and over the side of the bed she suddenly stopped, realising that neither her mum nor her dad knew anything about the Faeries she could see through the garden lantern, and with whom she regularly talked.

To say she talked with them was a strange way to put it, but she couldn't think of another way to describe it even to herself. In practice, she never spoke actual words to them. She would think of what she wanted to say to them and, somehow, they would hear it without her having to speak the words out loud at all. Sometimes, they would "say" something, and the thoughts would "appear" in her head. And then, she would answer them through thoughts of her own. The whole experience was very strange, but she always felt excited during and after it. It was simply very stimulating.

These 'conversations' were often about unusual things but also sometimes about very routine things. The Faeries would ask her about what she had been doing that day. Or they might ask her about what was happening where she lived, such as in her village or town, or even sometimes the country where she lived. They would always ask her if she wanted to know about them.

The first question Molly always asked them was, 'What are your names?" This was followed by, 'Where do you live?' and then 'Are your family or friends with you?' And she was almost always surprised by their answers. The names seemed strange to her. Recently she had 'spoken' with Mayfly, Maple Leaf, and Iris Flower. Once, she 'spoke' with Clematis.

Strangely, all the Faeries had the names of plants or flowers which she had heard her dad talk about in relation to their garden. It was more-or-less the same Faeries with whom she spoke each time through the lantern. So, she was becoming good friends especially with Mayfly, Maple Leaf and Iris Flower.

None of the Faeries ever seemed to want to answer any questions about where they lived, except to say, 'We live in a very different place to you. Our world includes elves, Faeries, unicorns, and others from The Land of Faerie. It is a special place, and we very much want you to keep in touch with us.' She had never had an answer to whether the Faeries had family or friends with them.

As she sat on the bed, Molly decided to try and get more information from her Faerie friends next time she spoke with them. She also said to herself, 'And I must tell them about the dream with all those other people and that I think I might know what could be causing the problem for everyone keeping in touch with The Land of Faerie, but I didn't have enough time to tell everyone.'

She then remembered that to do either of these things she would need the garden lantern to be working properly. Dad, she thought to herself. And in a flash, she was off the bed and going downstairs to see him. By the time Molly got downstairs, it was nearly dusk. Some of the house lights were already on.

Molly's Mum and Dad were sitting in the living room. The TV was on, and her mum was watching a quiz show which she watched every day. Her dad was reading the local evening newspaper.

"Dad?"

"Yes, Molly, what is it?" he replied, without looking up from his paper.

"Do you think the lantern will be working by now? It is getting quite dark outside so we should be able to see the light, shouldn't we?"

Her dad looked up from the newspaper and replied, "Well, you can go see, can't you? But if it isn't working properly yet, then don't get too upset. It might be too soon for the batteries and solar panels to have started to work fully. Let me know what you find."

At that, Molly turned and almost ran into the garden. She looked and looked and looked again but the lantern light was not even showing as a dull light or flickering. She walked slowly with her head down back into the living room.

"It isn't working Dad." She said in a very miserable tone of voice.

"Well, we should give it another 24 hours Molly and if it still isn't working by then we can take it to the DIY store and ask Mandy if she can explain it. How does that sound?" There was a pause, and then Molly said very quietly;

"OK Dad." She then went back upstairs to her bedroom, read one of her favourite books, and looked, from time-to-time down onto the lantern in the garden below. There was still no light showing from the lantern.

The following day passed very, very slowly as far as Molly was concerned. After breakfast she read some more of her book and then went for a ride on her bike around the close where they lived. After lunch, she went to see Tom and they talked almost all the time about the lantern and the Faeries. He was as eager to hear more about what was going on in The Land of Faerie as was Molly. He didn't have a lantern in his garden, so he relied on hearing news from Molly. Molly stayed for supper with Tom and his mum at their house, and then went home which was not very far away at the end of the Close. That evening Molly left it as long as possible before looking for the first time at the lantern. It was now dark. She looked from her bedroom window.

The lantern was giving out just an extremely low, dull, light which was almost impossible to see. Molly slumped down onto her bed. After watching the lantern through her bedroom window for a while, she went downstairs.

"It's working Dad, but hardly at all. I can barely see the light from my room."

"Hm. Well, seems like something isn't right. I'm not at work tomorrow so I think we should go and see Mandy at the store and take the lantern with us."

As soon as breakfast was finished, Molly was ready to go. She had already got the lantern from the garden, and it now stood on the hallway table near the front door. She was excited as she felt certain Mandy would have the answer to why the light was barely working.

When they got to the store, they found Mandy was busy with other customers so her dad suggested they go to the small café inside the store and have a drink. Molly shrugged her shoulders and said, "OK Dad." They sat where they could see Mandy talking with the other customers. To their surprise, she came straight to see them in the café as soon as she had finished with the other customers.

"Hello Mr Stevens. Hello Molly. Didn't expect to see you both so soon with the lantern. Is something wrong?"

"Hello Mandy. Well, yes there seems to be, but I think I better let Molly explain."

Molly then told Mandy about the light having started to work but giving out only a very dim light which was hard to see at all. She explained that it had been in its usual place in the garden for three days now, but the light didn't get any stronger.

"Well, if there is something wrong inside the light it shouldn't take me long to find it. After all, it has new rechargeable batteries and the solar panels seemed good when I last saw them. If I take the lantern to my small workshop here at the back of the store, I can test everything inside including all the wiring and connections. It won't take more than fifteen minutes. Are you happy for me to do that?"

"Yes, yes please Mandy!!" said Molly, almost but not quite shouting.

"Many thanks Mandy," said her dad in a much calmer and quieter voice. "We'll just stay here and have another coffee – or maybe an ice cream, eh Molly – until you return." He then handed the lantern to Mandy who disappeared along one of the store's aisles, turned left and disappeared towards the rear of the store.

15 minutes had passed and already Molly was fidgeting in her seat. She had had an ice cream

and a short walk around the café and some of the nearby aisles in the store, simply to pass the time. 20 minutes went by but still no sign of Mandy. As 25 minutes approached, Molly saw her coming down one of the aisles towards them in the café.

"Well," she said, as she pulled-up a chair from one, vacant, table to sit at theirs. "I have tested all parts of this lantern. It isn't at all complicated, so it was simple to do. What took me more time was testing the solar panels with different levels of direct light."

"This sounds like a long story Mandy. Do you want a warm or cold drink?"

"A coffee would be great Mr Stevens. Just milk, no sugar. Thank you."

"Anyway," she continued, "I tested them under extremely bright white light and all levels of brightness down to very low. What I found was that the panels, and the lantern, work fine when the outside light is very bright – like a great summer day here in this part of the UK. However, when the outside light is only slightly less bright than this, the light from the lantern becomes weaker until, as you saw it yesterday, Molly, it is extremely weak indeed."

Mr Stevens arrived back from getting Mandy's coffee and, sitting down, looked at Molly's perplexed face.

"I only heard parts of what you said Mandy, but I gather that the lantern doesn't work well unless the sunlight is very bright. Is that right?"

"It is Mr Stevens."

"But folks in our part of the world, and even in this part of our country, won't get bright sunshine very often at all during the year. So, you must get many complaints about lanterns like this."

"Well, we do get some Mr Stevens but to be honest, not that many." Mandy took another large sip of her coffee, "You see most people aren't that bothered about having a very bright light in their lantern. As long as they can see a light of some sort, swinging away in the garden, that seems to be good enough."

Throughout this conversation, Molly had been staring at the lantern sitting on the table in front of them. Once Mandy had explained the problem, Molly had begun to think back over recent months and how it could be that she had been able to see her Faerie friends through the very bright light in the lantern. She then remembered. There had been many weeks of very warm, and very sunny weather. In fact, it had been the sunniest and warmest two months on record for many years.

Suddenly, and out-of-the-blue, her thoughts began to turn to the folks in the dream who were from all over the world. It could not be the same for all of them, could it? Some were from cooler, even cold, parts of the world but others were from hot, dry, and very sunny countries. Yet, they all said they could not always use their gateways to The Land of Faerie and had not been able to do so for some time. She was then woken from these thoughts by her dad.

"Are you OK Molly? You're quiet."

"I'm OK Dad but I was just wondering about all the people I met recently who could also not use their gateways to their Fairy friends."

She realised straightaway, that not only had she told her dad about the Faeries but she had told Mandy too. She began to blush. Her dad took the opportunity to ask her again about the folks she met.

"So, what have they got to do with our lantern not working all the time, Molly? And, come to think of it, where and when did you meet these folks?"

Molly realised that it was now impossible to keep everything secret. Her dad was looking at her with a very questioning expression and, for that matter, so was Mandy.

"OK Dad. I said I would explain about the light once it was fixed so I will." She took a large gulp from her juice drink, but before she could start her explanation her dad interrupted.

"Hey. Mandy. You have done everything you can do with our lantern and I'm sure you don't have the time to sit here with us and hear Molly's story. We are really very thankful for all the time and effort you have put into our lantern."

"It so happens, Mr Stevens, that my shift here at the store just finished ten minutes ago. If you and Molly don't mind, I'd like to stay and hear Molly's story."

"Fine with me Mandy. OK with you Molly?"

"Sure. I'd like that."

"Off you go then Molly."

done.

Chapter Nine

"Well, the lantern arrived out of the blue. Mum won it in a raffle at the school. She is a teaching assistant in the ower School. That is where I used to be until last year when I moved to the Upper School.

"We didn't know what to do with it, but Mum decided it might look good hanging from one of the spare hooks on the bird feeder in the garden.

"It has a rechargeable light so that it can be seen at night in the garden. I think Mum said, it will look good.

"I never thought too much about it but after two or three nights I began to be drawn to the light which seemed to get brighter and brighter. I never thought that was because the sun was so strong.

"When I looked at the light it was just a light, but when I looked into it, I began to see moving objects or "things". It was difficult to say what they were.

"I didn't look at the light for a few days, but I was always wondering about it. When I went back to look at it I saw the 'moving things' again, but this time they weren't so much 'things' as like insects.

The nearest I can think of is dragonflies. I saw them as part of a biology lesson at school about different types of insects. They were beautiful. Many different colours and with very fine wings which it seemed to me I could almost see through."

Molly paused for a drink and took a big gulp. Mandy and her dad were clearly fascinated with her story so far, sitting quietly but Tom slightly forward showing their eagerness to hear the next instalment of the tale.

"The next night the dragonflies were there again but this time something weird happened. They began to speak to me. I didn't hear words, as such, nor could I see their mouths move, but the words came into my head somehow."

Molly's dad sat back in his chair as if he had lost interest in the story at this point. However, Mandy continued to look directly at Molly and was still Tom slightly forward towards her.

"The first words I heard, so to speak, were 'hello, my name is Maple Leaf. I am a Fairy. Who are you?'

"I was so shocked I didn't really know what to do. I began to think, 'Well, I am a young girl. My name is Molly Stevens and I live in England'.

As I thought these things, the dragonflies, or Faeries or whatever they were, began to move about more than before. They seemed excited.

"Since that night I have had regular talks with Maple Leaf and one or two others in the light. Until, that is, the light began to go dim. Before that, they told me that our light was what they called 'a gateway' between their world and ours or, to put it another way they said, 'between our world and theirs'. They told me there were many such gateways around our world and it seemed all of them had stopped working properly. Iris Flower said this did not happen all at once or even over the same time period, but gradually many gateways began to fail one way or another, and at different times. I wasn't sure what all this meant, and I'm still not sure I understand it."

Molly then looked at her dad, who by now was not in a very good mood to judge by his expression.

"Well, Dad, that's the story. I made good friends with the Faeries and that's why it is so important to me to have our lantern working properly. I think it is also important for the Faeries given what they said to me. They want to be in touch with humans but without the lights, or gateways as they call them, that is impossible."

Mandy leant back in her chair and smiled. "What an amazing story Molly. You have a remarkable imagination."

"Yes, you have, but this time I think your imagination has run riot young lady, to coin an old phrase."

"I haven't imagined any of it," Molly shouted, "I haven't. Next time the lantern is fully working you can come and see for yourself."

"OK Molly, OK. Now calm down and stop shouting. We will both come to see your Faeries or dragonflies or whatever they are. Is that OK with you Mandy?"

Mandy nodded.

"But," said Mr Stevens, "You still haven't explained about all the people you say you met who also have problems with their lights. Who are these people and where did you meet them, Molly?"

Molly was now quite deflated and looked down at the table. She knew it was going to sound very strange but all she could do was tell the truth. So, she described the dream she had had and what she heard the people in it say about their lights. She described some of the different clothes they were wearing and that she could recognise some of them from a couple of geography school lessons she had been in. By now, her dad was clearly fed-up hearing what he later described to Molly's mum as 'stuff and nonsense'.

"Well, come on Molly, we have been here far too long already. Time we went home." And at that he stood up from the table. Mandy hadn't said anything for quite some time but didn't feel she could let them go without saying what she thought was happening to their lantern, and all the others too.

"I know you're in a hurry to get off, but just before you go Mr Stevens, I have an idea about what might be causing your lantern to work properly only now and then."

"Please let us hear Dad, please?"

"OK Molly. Thanks Mandy but best if you can keep it short."

"Will do Mr Stevens. So, what has intrigued me about your lantern, and now with news that people around the world might be having similar problems with their garden lights, is what phenomenon could possibly cause this. Whilst Molly was talking, it occurred to me that it could be what is called 'Global Dimming'.

Mr Stevens screwed-up his face in a questioning sort of expression, and said, "Global Dimming? I've heard of 'global warming' of course, and you have too from school I know Molly – but global dimming. I've never heard of it."

"Well, in some ways it is related to 'global warming' Mr Stevens, but it is quite complicated to explain properly, and I know you are in a hurry.

"Oh, please Dad. Can't we just stay to hear what this thing is?"

"You can always look it up on the internet, Molly. You will find plenty of descriptions and explanations there. Anyway, I will write a summary about it and pop it through your letterbox at home later today or tomorrow morning before I start work. How does that sound?" Molly's shoulders dropped.

"There you are Molly your own 'research project' with your own research supervisor. How exciting is that? Anyway, come on we have to go. Thank you so much for all your time Mandy and for volunteering to write something for Molly. I'll be interested to find out what this 'global dimming' is all about myself."

Mr Stevens shook Mandy's hand and Mandy, in turn, gave Molly a huge hug. They all waved goodbye in the car park and went on their separate ways.

Chapter Ten

By the time they got home, Molly was both very excited and very tired. Her Mum had had their lunch ready for some time before they arrived. It was, thankfully, just a cold one of salads, cheeses and some cooked meats, with one of her homemade cakes afterwards. They all sat down together. Molly's Mum was eager to know what had kept them so long at the DIY store. She was going to ask Molly but seeing how tired she looked she decided to ask her husband instead.

"Well, the short version is that Mandy examined the lantern very thoroughly and then concluded there wasn't anything wrong with it." He then summarised what had happened after that – often, it has to be said, with a mouth partly full of food – including all the 'stuff and nonsense' as he put it, which Molly had told him and Mandy about the Faeries etc. He finished by saying that Molly had a small research project to discover more about 'global dimming'.

Throughout all of this, Molly had been eating as if she might not get any more food – ever. When she had finished, her mum said, "So, Miss Stevens, are you going to search the internet for 'global dimming'?

"Yes Mum. I'm off to my bedroom to do just that."

Her mum looked at her and smiled. It was what is often called 'a knowing smile'. What that meant is that her Mum didn't believe Molly would end-up searching the internet. What seemed more likely was that she would go upstairs, lie down on her bed just for a short rest and then go fast asleep. And that was, in fact, exactly what happened.

Molly awoke to a noise which she couldn't quite explain. As she lay on the bed, her Mum appeared in her bedroom and said, "Well, young lady, there is a letter for you. It just came through our letterbox."

"Ah. That was the noise I heard," said Molly. "It was the letterbox."

"You better come downstairs and see what it is, I think, don't you?"

Molly sat on the settee, opened the letter, and read it out loud.

"Dear Molly

It was great to spend so much time with you earlier today and to learn about your exciting times with your friends. I do hope you have been able to find out a few things about 'global dimming' since you got back home but I have tried to give you a short summary below of all the main things I know about this. I have made it as simple as I can and do hope it will be helpful. So, here we go.

Global dimming is thought to be due to the increased number of small particles in the Earth's atmosphere caused by dust, pollution, the eruptions of volcanoes, and even vapor trails from aircraft, and maybe other things. The more particles there are then the less sunlight gets through to us on the Earth's surface. In addition to this, another effect of having more small particles in the clouds is that water gathers around them creating lots more small water droplets (rain to you and me) which in turn makes the clouds more reflective – a bit like a mirror. That means they will reflect more sunlight back into space than they would otherwise do, so less of it reaches us on the Earth's surface.

As you will guess from this, I think Molly, the 'dimming effect' isn't the same everywhere. In some parts of the World, it is hardly noticeable and maybe especially in those places which have done a lot to reduce atmospheric pollution. In other places, it can be much more noticeable.

These things are all connected, one way or another, to 'global warming' but that is too complicated for this short message I am afraid.

Well, Molly, that is the best I can do in a quick note. I do hope it helps you with your project.

Please do say hello to your dad – it was great to meet him – and your mum.

With love and best wishes

Mandy"

Molly looked up from the notepaper and stared at her mum and then her dad. There was a long silence. Then, Molly's dad said, "Well, young lady, that is so helpful of Mandy, isn't it? Maybe you now have an explanation for not just why our lantern doesn't work properly all the time but why so many garden lights in different parts of the world don't either."

"It's hard to understand all the information Dad, but I know what you mean about explaining the problems with other outside lights around the world. But what do I do now I have all this information?"

Chapter Eleven

Unicorn had decided that there must be a way through the conundrum of what might connect the various lights around the world which did not work properly all of the time. He looked at everyone in 'The Gathering'. They were looking at him in anticipation that he was about to give them an answer to this question.

He was not sure why the Gathering might think he had the answers, except perhaps that it was true he spent a lot of time in the dreams of humans and might, therefore, have some answers. However, he didn't.

Suddenly, as if from nowhere, he heard his father's voice. It was a great shock. He hadn't heard the voice for many, many years – in human terms, many more than a hundred. Like elves and some others from the Land of Faerie, unicorns could speak without moving their lips.

'Hello Father. It is wonderful to hear your voice again. What do you want?'

'It is not what I want young unicorn, but what you need.'

'And what is that my father?'

'You need a way to find out what is the common thing linking all the gateways from elven folk to humans which are not working properly. Am I right?'

'You are, Father. Do you know the answer? Can you help?'

'I do not have the answer, but I know where you can find it.'

'And where is that Father?'

'The young human called Molly has the answer. You need to speak with her.'

'But how can I do that. She will need to dream of me before I can speak with her.'

There was a long pause – well, in human terms that is. Then, Unicorn's father said;

'Do you forget so quickly my son. Remember what your grandmother taught you when you were a much younger unicorn. She would have said that of all the skills we have, this one is probably the greatest of them all.'

And at that, Unicorn's father left his son's thoughts. He was gone.

Eventually, Unicorn looked up and, after a while, directly at The Gathering. The 'conversation' with his father had taken just a minute or less in human terms. The Gathering were all still looking, expectantly, at him.

'What is the greatest of all the skills I have? What IS it?'

He thought for what seemed to him an exceptionally long time. Then it came to him.

'Empathy. Yes, it is empathy, and of course that is the way to get in touch with Molly'. He then began to recall his grandmother's words when he was just a young unicorn – at least in unicorn terms.

'Empathy is when you can feel the thoughts, motives and feelings of another creature. It does not easily come my young grandson, nor can you have empathy with everyone. You need to practice it. But once you empathise with another, there is no feeling like it in the world – whether our world or that of other creatures.'

"You have been gone from us for a long time Unicorn," said Queen Carolina. She did not sound angry or frustrated, just curious. "May we know where you have been in your thoughts?"

Unicorn wondered what to say, but he had always been taught that honesty is the best policy. So, he said, "I have been talking with my father about the problem we have, my Lady Queen."

The Queen, Prince and Princesses looked at him with very curious expressions. Unicorn expected such a reaction.

"My father came to talk with me about our problem and gave me a clue as to a possible way forward." He then went on to describe 'empathy'.

The body language of the elven Prince and Princesses suggested they were unsure about this. Charlelot spoke for all of them when he said;

"Is it possible Unicorn? Can you reach-out to this human called Molly and find the answer we seek?"

"I am not sure my Prince, but I believe it must be worth trying. I do not have any other answers to our dilemma."

"Is there anything we can do to help you?" said Princess Josephina.

"Perhaps, my Princess. The strength of all our minds must be more powerful than mine alone. If I describe her to you and each of you focuses your mind on her, and gives her the same message, then maybe she will hear our call and meet me 'mind-to-mind'." Queen Carolina responded at once.

"I believe it is our best hope." She looked at the others who nodded their agreement – some more enthusiastically than others it has to be said.

"Good. So, what is the message you wish us all to give?"

Unicorn contacted each of them 'mind-to-mind' and said,

'Hello Molly. You need to contact Unicorn urgently. We need your help to put right the problems with the gateways. Just think of him very, very hard. Concentrate just on him.'

As soon as he had finished, each of them nodded and then drifted into a sort of trance, as they tried to connect Molly's mind to theirs.

Chapter Twelve

It was the strangest experience Molly could remember having at any time. She was with her good friend Tom when she heard the first one. However, to say she 'heard' it is not strictly accurate.

She and Tom were playing in Tom's back garden. It was a bat-and-ball game which Molly had always called French Cricket – though this wasn't strictly accurate either. In this game, one player has a small bat and the other a small soft ball or tennis ball. The player with the ball stands about two metres from the one with the bat and tries to hit the batter's legs by throwing the ball, underarm, at them. The bowler can move all around the batter, trying to outwit them about the direction from which the ball will come. A game ends after ten hits and then starts all over again. It can be great fun if played in the right spirit.

They were in the middle of their second game when she 'heard' the first voice. Molly didn't know but it was Princess Esmeralda of Eastern Wood, At first, she couldn't understand what was being said, but then another voice started saying the same things. Then there was another, and then another.

By the time the fourth voice was playing in her head Molly had dropped her bat and was already listening very intently to what was being said. Tom wondered what on earth was happening.

"Hey, Moll are you OK?" Molly really didn't like this shortened version of her name and if anyone other than Tom used it, she would tell them so 'in no uncertain terms' as the saying goes.

"Er, yes, thanks Tom. I'm OK. I just have these strange sounds in my head. I'm not sure what they are but they sound like voices. They are quite faint so it's hard to tell." It was very unusual for Molly to stop playing this game in the middle, and Tom was both curious and concerned.

"What are they saying? Who are they?"

"Well, they seem to be saying something about the unicorn. You know, the one we saw in that weird dream."

"What about him?"

"I'm not sure, but I think I'm supposed to think about him and then, well...er...hmm..."

"What then?" said Tom, who was not now just curious and concerned but also confused.

"I don't know," Molly said sharply. "Anyway, I've had enough playing our game. I'm off home. It must be almost time for my tea, anyway."

Tom was disappointed but he could see that Molly was distracted by all these noises or voices, or whatever they were, in her head. "OK. See you tomorrow if you survive the ghosts," he said, with a very broad grin.

"Ha. Ha. Ha," Molly said in a voice like her mum's when she was getting at Molly, and then began to make her way home.

Molly now had so much going on in her head it was truly 'spinning', as another saying goes. She kept hearing the voices talking about unicorn, and she couldn't stop recalling the note from Mandy about "global dimming". She played it all over and over in her mind as she walked home. By the time she got there, she had a plan.

She went into the house through the back door; said "Hello, Mum" as she disappeared into the hallway from the kitchen, and then up the stairs to her bedroom.

"Good to see you again Ms Stevens," her Mum shouted after her, somewhat sarcastically. "Your tea will be ready in 15 minutes so don't be late."

"OK Mum. I won't," came the distant, shouted, reply from Molly's bedroom.

Molly's plan was to try and find out which parts of the world were the most polluted before she tried to contact Unicorn. If she was going to ask for help from him, or the Faeries, she had to have something to ask them to do.

She sat on her bed with her tablet and started to search for "the world's most polluted countries". There were many sources, but she eventually settled on one, with the most recent information, which ranked the countries from "worst" to "best". Inevitably, she searched first for the UK. It was listed at No.92 out of just over 100 places. So, it seemed, along with France (72), Spain (80), Australia (95), Canada (97), and Sweden (103) it wasn't doing too badly, relatively speaking.

In contrast, Bangladesh (1), Pakistan (2), India (3), Oman (6), Qatar (7), Bosnia Herzegovina (10), and China (14) weren't doing very well at all. Some other countries she noticed in the list were Mali (13), Chile (42), Italy (47), South Africa (49), Peru (50), and Kenya (67).

Molly had no idea whether this information about any of these countries would be of use to Unicorn. After all, she had no idea where the problem lights, or gateways, were located around the world. What she did know was that the UK wasn't doing too badly in trying to reduce air pollution compared to some other places.

'So, maybe the Faeries have had problems 'talking' through the gateways with their human friends in those places for some time, and only recently with our lantern.' As she thought about this, she heard her mum's voice calling up the stairs.

"OK Mum. Just coming."

Chapter Thirteen

The Prince, Princesses and Queen continued their attempts to communicate with Molly for what seemed to them to be a very long time. However, we must bear in mind that time in the Land of Faerie passes very quickly compared to time for us humans. A few minutes for elves, pixies and other creatures in that mystical land seems like weeks to them. A few minutes for us is little more than a blink of the eye, as the phrase goes. So, while Molly was having her tea and deciding what she should do about the voices, The Gathering was becoming restless and concerned that what Unicorn had suggested would never work. Unicorn sensed the unease among the elves.

He addressed them, which was a very unusual thing for a unicorn to do without being invited to do so by an elven Queen, if there was one present. He looked directly at Queen Carolina though his words were meant for everyone present

"We must all try to be patient. It is sadly true that I have not had any contact from the human called Molly. But we must bear in mind that time here passes very differently from time in the human world. I have discovered this many times in their dreams. Time in their dreams passes erratically but it often still passes much more slowly than in our world."

meant for everyone present

"We must all try to be patient. It is sadly true that I have not had any contact from the human called Molly. But we must bear in mind that time here passes very differently from time in the human world. I have discovered this many times in their dreams. Time in their dreams passes erratically but it often still passes much more slowly than in our world."

The elves began to talk in whispered voices among themselves even as the Prince, Princesses and the Queen continued to focus their thoughts on Molly. Unicorn began to wonder himself if they would succeed in encouraging her to contact him. Then, quite suddenly, he "heard", in his mind rather than as speech, a very faint "voice". Could it be that Molly had sensed their unease and suddenly decided to contact him?

At first, he could not understand what was being conveyed to him. He was not even sure it was Molly. It could have been any human. He turned to face Queen Carolina once again.

"My lady, I think Molly may be trying to make a connection with me. I will now try to listen very carefully. If it is Molly, I will nod my head three times to you, and the Prince, Princesses and your Gracious Self can stop your strenuous efforts to contact her."

Queen Carolina nodded to Unicorn. At that, he walked very slowly a few paces from The Gathering and concentrated on the "voice" now filling his head.

Unicorn concentrated very, very hard but the words coming into his head were muffled. It was as if a human was speaking out of their mouth through a sock or was eating as they spoke. Unicorn had to be patient. He waited. Then quite suddenly, the words became clearer.

"Hello Mr Unicorn. This is Molly. It is important we speak about the gateways I think?"

Unicorns do not normally show emotions but at hearing these words in his mind, Unicorn became quite emotional. A small tear trickled down his cheek. He turned towards the Queen and nodded three times. She nodded once in return and with a large smile.

"Hello Molly. Yes, you are correct. Can you tell me why so many of them are failing?"

There was a very long pause -well, for a Unicorn – and then he heard words he did not want to hear at this moment.

"I have lots of information, but first please will you tell me who were all those other voices in my head?"

Unicorn hesitated. He needed to try and convey the seriousness with which The Land of Faerie was considering these latest events, but he did not want to extend this "mind-to-mind" connection too long with Molly. Afterall, this is not the way humans normally communicate. She was a young human, and he believed such a connection might be very tiring for her. He decided to keep it very short.

"They were Faerie Princes and Princesses who agreed to try and contact you all together to help our chances."

Unicorn waited. And waited. And waited some more. Then;

"Mr Unicorn. It seems that we have a problem with sunlight getting to our world. In some places it is not so bad but in others it is very bad".

Molly was now in her bedroom, after her tea, and working her brain overtime to try and find thoughts – as this is what they were for her – which could send simple messages to Unicorn.

So, what might this have to do with the gateways?, Unicorn thought to himself. He did not understand. He decided to ask Molly that exact question. Once again, there was a long pause. But by now, Molly was becoming more used to this "speaking mind-to-mind", and realised she had to try and keep the statements or questions very short. So, she said

"Well, Mr Unicorn, it seems that many of the outdoor lights around our world, which are our gateways, rely on sunlight to recharge themselves. This can be a problem in some places".

Unicorn wrestled with this idea.

"So, what can we do about this, Molly?"

Once again, there was what seemed to him a very long pause before he heard anything from Molly. Then he heard the words he hoped he would never hear.

"I am sorry Mr Unicorn. I do not know."

Chapter Fourteen

Unicorn had been right when he guessed that communicating mind-to-mind would probably be tiring for a young human like Molly. After she had sent her message that she did not know how they could solve the problem with the gateways, she soon sensed that Unicorn was no longer connected with her, so to speak. She waited a short time and once it was clear to her that he had "switched-off" she collapsed backwards on her bed. She was exhausted and in only a few moments, fast asleep.

She woke in what seemed to her only a few moments later, to the sound of her dad's voice.

"Molly? Are you OK up there?" He was calling from the hallway below her bedroom. He and Molly's Mum had never heard Molly so quiet playing with her toys, and it had been almost two hours since she went to her bedroom after tea.

Molly rubbed both her eyes with her fingers and gave a long and wide yawn.

"Yes Dad, I am fine. I think I dozed-off after tea just like you do after lunch some days," she said with a huge grin, as she knew it irritated him when her mum commented on him "having a nap" as he called it.

"You're a cheeky monkey young Ms Stevens," he said, also with a broad smile on his face, though of course Molly couldn't see that. "If you want to stay up there until bedtime that's fine but there are some good programmes on TV tonight, remember?"

Molly was still trying to clear her mind. What was on TV wasn't anywhere in her consciousness just now.

"OK Dad. Thanks. I'll stay here for a while and maybe come down later."

"Alright, but don't forget there is a programme on tonight at nine o'clock about global warming. I thought you might be interested in that, and your mum, and I agreed you could stay up a little later than normal to watch it if you wanted to." Molly replied instantly.

"Yes, Dad, I do want to watch it very much. I'll be down in time to watch it."

Chapter Fifteen

Even as he heard Molly's words in his mind, he knew he would have to tell The Gathering what she had said. This was not something he wanted to do. He was aware of the tensions among the elves about the importance which some placed on making and keeping contact with the human world. He could foresee those tensions erupting again almost as soon as he told them what Molly had said. Still, he felt he had no choice but to tell them. He looked up at The Gathering which was a few paces from where he stood. All eyes were fixed upon him. He spoke, using normal speech directly to the Queen, though he knew all assembled there would be able to hear him.

"My Gracious Queen. I have had a good mind-to-mind conversation with the young human called Molly. She told me she has a lot of information about what is causing the gateways between our two worlds to fail." At this, many of the elves shuffled forward a little, clearly eager to hear what Unicorn would say next.

"Please do continue Sir Unicorn. I think you can see how interested we all are in what she went on to say." Unicorn knew he could not avoid the issue any longer.

"Molly told me, my Queen, that many of the outdoor lights around her world, which are their gateways to our world, rely on sunlight to recharge themselves and that this is proving to be a problem in some places." The elves began to whisper to each other such that there was an increasing murmuring sound around the woodland glade where they were gathered. The Queen raised her right hand slowly into the air and the murmuring stopped almost instantly.

"Dear friends, I know this message sounds strange and, indeed, I do not understand it all myself. However, I fear there is more to come from Sir Unicorn." Unicorn swallowed hard and said;

"Sadly, there is my Lady Queen. I asked Molly what we could do about this problem, and she replied that she was sorry, but she didn't know."

The murmuring among The Gathering broke out once more, though now it was much louder than before. Once again, Queen Carolina raised her right hand with her palm facing the gathered elves.

"I had understood Sir Unicorn that your father had said that this young human called Molly would have the answer to our problem with the gateways to their world. Did I misunderstand? Unicorn needed to be careful. It was not every day, or even every hundred years, that a Unicorn corrects a Queen. He chose his words carefully.

"You did not misunderstand my Queen, but my father advised we needed to know what it was which linked the gateways and was causing many of them to fail. It was this common link which, I believe, he thought the young Molly could identify for us."

"And she has said it is a problem with sunlight not reaching some of them so they cannot recharge themselves? Am I right?

"You are, my Queen."

"But what is this thing called 'recharging'? For me, recharging is about the 'Bull God' charging and charging again to beat-off the enemies of our Land as happened seven thousand years ago. Does this young human know about the Bull God? And what does the Bull God have to do with lights in the human world?"

Unicorn had to admit to himself that he too had no idea what Molly had meant when she told him about sunlight recharging the lights. His empathic insights made it clear to him, however, that this was not about the Bull God.

"I do not believe that the word 'recharging' has anything to do with the Bull God, my Lady. I do not, however, know what it is about." Unicorn now took a gamble. He had been thinking about this from the moment his mind and Molly's disengaged from each other and now, he judged, was the time to share his thoughts with The Gathering. He said;

"My connection with Molly was based around my empathy with her. We had met in her dreams many times and with that experience behind me I felt sure I could become empathetic with her. My feelings about her after this empathetic connection are very powerful. I do believe she may not yet have the answers we seek but she is trying to find them."

At this point, and quite unexpectedly, Prince Charlelot stepped forward to speak. Queen Carolina half-bowed towards him as a sign that she was granting him permission to speak to The Gathering.

"My Gracious Lady Queen, Princesses, Sir Unicorn, attendant fellow Elves. I have always been, as you know, a strong supporter of maintaining contact with the human world, or 'The Other World' as some in Northern Wood refer to them." A gentle ripple of soft applause ran through the attendant elves from Northern Wood at this point. He continued;

"Through the efforts of you my Queen, our Princesses, and Sir Unicorn, we now know what the problem is that is shared by the gateways. Surely, this is as far as we need to go. Those in the human world who want to communicate with us, can do so through their children's' stories and their dreams.

I believe I speak for the Northern Wood elves here, and probably many still in Northern Wood, that we do not need to take the matter of the gateways any further. Let the humans solve it if they wish to."

Many elves from around The Gathering, and not just those from Northern Wood, applauded softly.

Queen Carolina looked at Esmeralda and Josephina. Her gaze made it clear to them – but to no one else – that she was looking for advice. Perhaps even guidance. One by one, they "spoke" to Carolina "mind-to-mind".

Josephina said, "I do not believe our elves understand that the connection with humans is more than just something which is 'nice to have' but something which is essential to our survival"

Esmeralda said, "My Sister Princess is right. Somehow, we must now make sure the elves in each of our domains understands the importance of our regular contact with the human world. We have for too long kept this a close secret. Now they must know."

Carolina replied very quickly. "You are right my sisters, and I thank you for this powerful reply to my call. I will now reply to Charlelot and make it clear that I hope the message will pass from this Gathering out across the whole Wood. If you are content with this, just nod."

Both Princesses nodded and immediately the Queen addressed the Gathering.

"My dear Prince Charlelot, and Elves from all corners of our Wood. These are complex times, and it seems clear there are some problems with the gateways we use to the human world, and they use to ours, which will be difficult to overcome." The Gathering fell eerily silent.

"Many of us here have had good experiences through contact with humans in their dreams. Those of you who have not yet had that pleasure should look forward to it." At this point her eyes settled on some younger elves among the elves accompanying the Prince and Princesses – younger meaning less than two hundred years old in elvish years.

"However, I do know that some here today – and probably some or even many still in our home woods – question whether it is sensible for us to make so much effort to keep in contact with the human world. I can tell you, it is not only sensible, but also essential to our survival."

The earlier murmuring began again, and even louder than before. Unicorn started to wonder what the Queen was about to say, but he guessed and wondered what would happen after she had explained the situation. He stood, head slightly bowed, and simply listened.

"You see our lives here in The Land of Faerie, are very closely linked with those of humans." The Queen stood quite still and waited for a short time. "You see, humans created us in their imaginations. We are – I am sorry to tell you – no more nor no less than what humans have created in their minds. If we allow humans to forget about us, then gradually we will cease to exist."

The still, quiet, amongst the assembled groups lasted for a very short time and then there was an audible intake of breath among them. The silence resumed. A stunned silence not an expectant one. The Queen continued.

"It is, therefore, in all of our interests to do whatever we can to make sure humans do not forget about us. Yes, we could rely on them reading about us in their books as children, but this places all the emphasis on human children continuing to remember us – to think about us – when they become older. Sadly, we know from our experience with human dreams that it is overwhelmingly children who dream about us and rarely adults." At this point, she looked directly at Unicorn, hoping he would affirm what she had said from his very long experience of human dreams.

With his head bowed, Unicorn did not see the Queen turn to look at him. However, he sensed her gaze and so he looked up and met her eyes with his. The Queen did not need to say anything for

Unicorn to understand what she was hoping for. So, he said;

"You are right, my Queen. Over many hundreds of years experiencing human dreams, it has indeed been very rare for me to meet older humans or adults as they call themselves."

The Queen inwardly smiled to herself and then, turning back to look at the Gathering, she said;

"Enabling humans to see us as living beings, and to talk with us, through their gateways clearly makes us much more real to them than any number of words or even pictures in a book. With our human friends, we must find a solution to the problem with the gateways."

It was very unusual for the Queen to raise her voice as she did when stressing "must" in her final sentence. Some of the elves even jumped when they heard it. All of them, without exception, were shocked and surprised at the message she had given them. The elves from the Northern Wood were shocked far more than anyone would have expected given they had always opposed making efforts to keep in touch with the human world. Their usual light pale skin colour was now almost pure white.

The Gathering was still coming to terms with what Queen Carolina had said and stood in complete silence looking at her. As they did so, Princess Josephina "spoke" mind-to-mind with the Queen.

She did it in such a way that her sister Princess, Esmeralda, could "hear" too.

"My noble Queen. Your words were brilliantly chosen and very powerfully delivered, which is exactly what we needed at the crossroads our world now faces. Our attendant companies seem to be still in a state of shock. Might I suggest that whilst they are still feeling the full force of your words, we send one or more messengers back to our respective woods to convey the message to all other elves?" Princess Esmeralda nodded enthusiastically at this suggestion. Queen Carolina replied almost instantly.

"This is an excellent suggestion my sisters. However, I think Charlelot must also be told what is happening. We must ensure all the elves in Northern Wood understand that their objections to making ever greater efforts to keep in contact with humans must now end. The problem we face needs effort by all creatures in the Great Wood" The two Princesses nodded towards the Queen.

"So, with that in mind and before I speak with Prince Charlelot, I will speak with Sir Unicorn. He will be a very important friend and powerful ally in our struggle to solve the problem with the gateways." The two Princesses nodded again.

Immediately, Queen Carolina started to "speak" mind-to-mind with Unicorn. Her words fell into his mind like Autumn leaves dropping onto a lake from an overhanging tree.

"Ah. My Queen. What can I do for you? I imagine it has to do with the gateways?"

"Yes, it does Sir Unicorn. You will have seen and heard the reaction of the Gathering to my message, I am sure. The Princesses and I believe it is now important to bring all creatures in The Great Wood to understand the importance of helping us to retain contacts with the human world. And we want to make sure all elves will do the same. After you and I have spoken I will contact Prince Charlelot about Northern Wood. After that, we will send messengers from The Gathering to the four corners of the Wood to give the message everyone heard today from me. So, will you help to take the message to creatures far and wide throughout the Wood? Will you bring your powers to bear on our quest if called upon?"

Unicorn listened very carefully to what the Queen said to him, but it did not take him long to reply.

"I will do whatever I can to help you with the quest my Queen, and I will also work hard to make sure every creature in The Great Wood knows the message you gave today".

The Queen smiled at the unconditional love which came through Unicorn's words and then turned her focus onto Prince Charlelot.

"Hello my brother."

There was no reply. The Queen tried again.

"Hello my brother. Are you well?"

The Queen was very disturbed by the fact there was no reply to her mind-to-mind greeting. Normally, this would only happen for two reasons: the creature concerned was unconscious or had "passed beyond" as the elves called it, or dead as humans call it. She tried one more time.

"Hello my brother."

She waited and waited and then, suddenly, she heard;

"Hello Carolina."

"Are you all right Prince Charlelot?" Again, the response was very slow in coming.

"I am fine my Queen, but I am surrounded by my elven folk from the Northern Wood who are talking endlessly, and loudly, about the speech you gave. I cannot, literally, hear myself think!!!!!!" The Queen smiled, and said;

"And from what you have heard them say so far, good Prince, do you think they will join the rest of The Great Wood to find a solution to the problems with the gateways?"

Once again there was a long pause.

"I believe so my Queen."

Queen Carolina did not like such an uncertain answer. ALL the energy in The Great Wood – or as much of it as possible – would be needed to solve this problem and make sure the connection between The Land of Faerie and the human world would be back to normal.

"We are sending messengers from The Gathering to Southern, Eastern and Western Woods to try and make sure every elf understands the importance of our contacts with the human world. If it would help you, I will come to Northern Wood to address your kinsfolk. What do you say?"

Prince Charlelot was now on the horns of a dilemma: accept the Queen's offer and, in effect, admit he could not control his Northern Elves. Or thank her, say she was always welcome in Northern Wood, but he felt all would be well without her presence this time. And then? The Northern Wood might well go on its own...possibly into oblivion. Inevitably, with the uncertainty in his mind, there was another long pause before he answered the Queen.

The Queen had never waited so long for a reply to an offer for her to attend any part of The Great Wood. Then Charlelot said;

"Your offer is very generous my Queen. I would be delighted to welcome you to my home in Northern Wood and provide an opportunity for you to address my kinsfolk. Thank you."

It could seem that so many mind-to-mind conversations would take many minutes. In fact, they took barely two.

The Queen and the two Princesses once again became conscious of The Gathering. There was a great deal of chattering between elves from the same areas of The Great Wood, and between elves from different areas or woods within it.

Chapter Sixteen

"It's on!!!!"

Molly heard her dad's words like a bolt out of the blue. She hadn't exactly forgotten about the programme on climate change, but the time had passed so quickly.

"OK Dad. Coming."

Molly ran out of her bedroom and down the stairs – skidding down them on her heels as she was in such a hurry. She landed on her bottom and, as she rubbed it, walked quickly into the living room. She sat down carefully in her favourite place on the settee for watching the TV, just after the programme started.

Molly wasn't that interested in all "the guff" as her dad called it, about global warming. She wanted to know why there was a problem with sunlight getting through to some parts of the world, at some times, compared to how it used to be. The first part of the Programme summarised an answer to the question, "what is global warming?" The presenter summarised the answer, helped by various scientists along the way.

"Since the Industrial Revolution from, let's say for convenience 1780, the overall temperature of the Earth has increased by just over one degree

Celsius. Over the hundred years from 1880 (the year accurate records started) to 1980, the Earth's temperature rose on average by 0.07 degrees Celsius every decade. However, since then the rate of temperature rise has nearly doubled. These rises in temperature may not sound very much at all. So, why all the fuss? Well, we now live on a planet that has never been hotter. And the impact of that is felt almost right across the globe – with increased melting of the ice caps in the Arctic and Antarctic; rising sea levels affecting many islands; more frequent, and more powerful, storms; more wildfires; extreme droughts and tropical storms. In a nutshell, global warming.

At this point, the programme stopped to go to a "commercial break".

Molly had read or heard all of this before, either in books or from her geography teacher at school. The programme was only on the TV for forty-five minutes and twenty of them had passed already. Being quite an impatient young woman, she began to wonder if the programme would have time to explain "global dimming". She fidgeted on the settee. Her Dad glanced at her and raised his eyes towards the ceiling.

The programme re-started and continued to explain global warming and its effects if humanity does nothing about it.

"I know all this, Dad. I've heard it, or read it, many times before. When will they talk about global dimming?"

"I don't know Molly. I hope..."

He was suddenly stopped in his tracks, so to speak, by the programme presenter mentioning the phrase global dimming.

"Listen Molly. Listen."

"But alongside global warming we have had a process which seems, on the face of it, to contradict or even counteract global warming. That is global dimming."

Molly bounced up and down on the settee much to her Mum's, and Dad's, annoyance as it was only a few months old and had been quite expensive. Still, they could not deny Molly's enthusiasm, smiled to each other, and said nothing.

The presenter continued;

"Global dimming is a decrease in the amount of direct sunlight which reaches the Earth's surface. Scientists have known about this since the 1950s when careful measurements first started. The effect is not the same everywhere across the world, but it can be as much as a 20% reduction in sunlight in some places."

"This is it, Dad. This is it!! This is what I wanted to hear."

"Then be quiet and listen young lady."

Molly looked sheepish but then straight back at the TV. The presenter continued;

"It is thought global dimming is caused by pollution affecting the Earth's atmosphere. Dust and other particles make clouds more reflective. So, more sunlight is reflected into space so less of it reaches the Earth. Some of these particles attract water droplets and lead to increased rainfall. However, from about 1990 this effect began to reverse especially over Europe owing to decreases in pollution through the efforts of many countries to reduce global warming. The reversal has not been the same everywhere in the world but the more that countries reduce airborne pollution, the more the dimming effect will reduce."

There was another "commercial break" at this point and Molly leapt straight from the settee and went directly to the downstairs loo. She came back just in time to hear the presenter conclude her piece on global dimming.

"It might seem that a process which reduces the effect of the sun on warming of the Earth would help with global warming, but the reality is that the more we reduce airborne pollution the less dimming effect there is and so, inevitably, the greater the effect of the sun we have to endure. Is this the Catch 22 of all Catch 22s?" At this point, the programme's title and end music began to play.

Molly sat on the settee and stared at the TV.

"Dad? What is a 'Catch 22'?"

Her dad gave her mum a 'knowing look' as it is sometimes called. He didn't say anything, but his expression said it all, and as much to say, 'I knew this would come up as soon as the TV presenter used the phrase'.

"Well young lady, the phrase comes from the title of a famous book by an American writer Joseph Heller. A "Catch-22" is a problem which is impossible to solve because the problem itself has aspects which make it impossible to solve." Molly stared at her dad.

"What does that mean?" her mum looked up from her newspaper and said;

"C'mon love. You're going to have to do better than that. What about using an example? And not the one from the book either. That is even more difficult to follow – well, for me at any rate." Molly's dad stared into the distance searching his mind for an example that Molly might be able to understand.

"OK Molly," he eventually said. "Suppose I lost something that was very dear to me. My natural reaction would be to start looking for it, wouldn't it?"

Molly nodded.

"But suppose what I have lost is my spectacles, or glasses as you call them. In this situation, it is very hard for me to look for what I've lost, or if my eyesight is very poor it may be impossible to do so with any chance of success. This is a Catch 22. If you like, it's a no-win situation."

Molly sat with each elbow resting on each knee, her head cupped in her hands and staring down from the settee at the floor. She looked gloomy but also thoughtful. Several minutes passed without any sound from her. Then, just as her dad was about to ask if she was alright, she said;

"So, if we try our hardest to cut back on all the things which produce greenhouse gases – which all the scientists say we must do – then we reduce global warming but also reduce global dimming. And if we do that, then the planet will heat-up even more."

Her dad smiled at her and then at his wife.

"Seems to be what they were saying at the end of that programme, Molly. But it is now way past your bedtime, so I think it's time for you to get some water to take with you and off upstairs to bed."

Molly didn't complain. She was very tired but

also had so many things whizzing around her head. She kissed her mum and dad goodnight and, after getting a glass of water from the kitchen, trudged slowly upstairs to bed.

Despite being very tired and really, really wanting to go to sleep, Molly found it impossible to get all the words and ideas about the gateways to go away. Was there anything that her friends in the Other World might be able to do, to solve the Catch 22?

Chapter Seventeen

The Gathering began to disband, but before it did the Faerie Queen Carolina addressed those chosen to be the Messengers across the Great Wood. Unicorn stood next to the Prince and Princesses as she spoke.

"Elves of The Gathering chosen as our Messengers. This night you carry an important burden. It is your great task to explain to your kinsfolk in each of your woods, and to all creatures there and elsewhere, the message I gave to all here not very long ago. All elves and all other creatures in our world must help in the Great Quest – as we will from this day name it – to solve the problems with our gateways to the human world." There was complete silence.

"Our great friend and ally in this quest, Sir Unicorn, will help us to also ensure as many creatures as possible in The Great Wood know of the problem and help them see how they can help us to solve it. He will also communicate with one young human whom we believe might hold the key to the answer we seek." Unicorn nodded.

"So, our Messengers, go to the four corners of this, our Great Wood. I wish you all the speed you need and all good fortune in your task. You go with

my blessing. And tell anyone who might ask, that you do."

At that, the Messengers said brief farewells to the elves who they would next see back in their home wood some days after they had left The Gathering. Elves are comfortable to show emotion, and these were, for some, emotional farewells.

As the Messengers left and the rest of the Gathering started preparing to disperse too, Unicorn took the opportunity to speak with Queen Carolina, the Prince and Princesses.

"My Lady Queen. I think it is important that I try to communicate with Molly."

"And why do you think that Sir Unicorn?"

"My 'human senses', as I call them, are telling me very strongly that she wants to communicate with me. I have never felt such a strong inclination before."

"In that case Sir Unicorn, it is what you must do. And we all hope that Molly has information which will help us in the Great Quest."

At that, Unicorn bowed and retreated several paces back from the Queen, the Prince, and the Princesses. It was not long before his outline became blurred and faint. In another moment, he was gone.

Chapter Eighteen

Molly had eventually gone to sleep and, of course, still with Unicorn and the Other World, as she called it sometimes, on her mind. Unsurprisingly, it was not long before she found herself in a dream in the Great Wood. She looked around but couldn't see Unicorn, elves, or any other folk. All was quiet.

Then, as if from nowhere, Unicorn appeared about 60 or 70 metres in front of her. He was grazing on the grasses beneath the trees. At first, he did not seem to notice her. She was about to say something but, as the saying goes, 'he beat her to it'.

He looked up straight in her direction. His wonderfully friendly, deep-blue, eyes stared at her.

"Ah. Molly. I was hoping we might meet soon."

"And I was hoping very much that we would too, Mr Unicorn."

"Do you have something more to tell me about the problems with the gateways, Molly?"

At this point, Molly wanted to say something positive and sensible, but she knew that all she could say would probably sound like nonsense to Unicorn.

"We have spoken before about the problem with sunlight not getting to some of our gateways, I think, Mr Unicorn."

"Yes, we have Molly, but we did not know how to solve the problem."

"Well, it seems the problem is very complicated Mr Unicorn. You see, our world has a big problem because it is getting hotter and hotter. The way to solve this is to stop us humans producing so many nasty things – called 'greenhouse gases' – which pollute our atmosphere. But if we try our hardest to cut back on all the things which make the greenhouse gases – which all the scientists say we must do – then we reduce global warming but also reduce global dimming. And if we do that, then the planet will heat-up even more."

Unicorn looked long and hard at Molly. He did not understand all the words, so he asked Molly what she meant by 'global dimming'?

"It is, I believe Mr Unicorn, what has been causing the problem with some of the gateways. It is when not enough sunlight can get through to our world, so the gateways cannot recharge their batteries. When that happens, they have no light."

Unicorn thought hard.

"But if what you say is happening then will this problem not go away as you reduce the gases?"

Molly smiled to herself. Unicorn was a very clever animal.

"It should be getting better already Mr Unicorn, but it will take a long time for the lights which are most badly affected to become normal again."

Unicorn's mind was working overtime.

"So, Molly, what if we, in this world, could provide the light which is needed for you to be able to link with us?"

Molly's eyes opened wider and wider. Her mouth kept opening and closing as if she was trying to say something, but no words came out. After a while, she began to get some words to come from her mouth;

"B...b...bu...but is it possible?"

Unicorn smiled both outwardly and inwardly. It was a beautifully warm and loving smile.

"There are many creatures and beings in Our World, Molly, which have special skills and powers. Humans, I think, call them magical. To us, they are simply the skills we were born with or have learned over many, many years."

By now, Molly had recovered from the surprise of what Unicorn had said. She was now thinking more clearly.

"So, Mr Unicorn, it could be possible to er...how would you say...send the light when our gateways have not been able to recharge?"

Unicorn lowered his head slightly and stared at the ground for a short time. Then, he raised his head, looked straight at Molly, and said, "If we know which gateways need light from us, and when they need it, then it is possible."

Molly clapped her hands and jumped up and down on the spot. She was so very excited. Unicorn smiled again – in fact, he almost seemed to start laughing in human terms – but he knew already there was a problem looming ahead with this idea.

"One thing we must do Molly, is agree how My World will be told by humans in Your World that they need us to provide light, and to which gateways." Molly stopped jumping up and down and clapping and began to look, once again, very miserable.

"But how can we do that, Mr Unicorn?"

Unicorn sensed that Molly's dream was coming to an end, so he said "We need to think more about this Molly. You and I will meet in another dream when we know the answers."

As he said these words, Molly had already started to become less clear to see. She was starting to wake up or, maybe, drift into a different dream. Unicorn moved away from where she was standing and in only the blink of an eye – as the saying goes – she was gone.

Unicorn knew he had much work to do, and he needed to start immediately.

Chapter Nineteen

Molly woke to the sound of her mum shouting to her. It was getting louder each time she spoke.

"Molly, Tom is here. He wants to speak with you about the lantern." Getting no reply, she was walking up to Molly's bedroom and saying the same words repeatedly as she went. Then, she was in the bedroom.

Molly was rubbing her eyes and trying hard to wake up. She had had a busy night in the Great Wood.

"C'mon Ms Stevens up you get. It is after nine already. Tom is downstairs in the living room."

"OK. Thanks Mum." She yawned. "I'll be down as soon as I am dressed."

"Well, don't be too long young lady."

Molly went into the living room to see Tom standing by the fire. "Hello sleepy head," he said, with a broad grin. Molly just stared at him and then said;

"So, what do you want to say about the lantern?" as she flopped down onto the settee.

"Well, why don't you use ordinary batteries in the lantern instead of the type which recharge through the solar panel?" Molly suddenly became wide awake. She hadn't thought of this and was annoyed with herself that it had taken Tom to point out such a simple solution. Nevertheless, she wasn't going to admit that to him.

"I know that would possibly work, Tom," she said in a very superior voice, "But it isn't the green way to run a garden light, is it? And it is also expensive. I don't think my dad would be too happy if I suggested it to him."

"Well, it was my dad who suggested it to me Moll."

"Will you pleeeese stop calling me that? You know I hate it as do my mum and dad." Tom sort of nodded, but it wasn't very convincing.

"And in any case our lantern isn't the only one having the problem. There are hundreds, or even thousands, around the world which have the same problem. Some of them could be owned by poor families who certainly couldn't afford ordinary batteries all the time. And anyway, I thought you were all for 'green' answers to the world's problems. You keep saying so in school."

Tom looked at her and then down at the floor. He knew she was right, at least on the last point. Molly sensed she was winning and so went in for the coup de grace – the final winning shot."

"Anyway, Unicorn has told me that our friends in the Great Wood can provide all the lanterns with the light they need when the sunlight isn't enough." She smiled a long, self-satisfied, smile.

"OK, so everything is fixed then, Molleeee." Tom emphasised the final sound of her name just, really, to score a point.

Molly wondered whether to tell Tom of the problem she and those in The Land of Faerie had. That is, how those in our world who had lights not working because of limited sunlight could tell those in the Great Wood. She decided she must. After all, Tom (or his mum or dad) might have the answer.

"Well, only partly Tom. You see, we need some way to tell those in The Land of Faerie which lanterns, or gateways, have the problem so they can be sure to use their magic to help those who need it."

By now, Tom was sat in an armchair facing Molly on the settee. He squirmed about in the chair trying to think of an answer. There was a long pause.

"Isn't that an easy one Molly?" he said.

"OK. Go on then."

"Well, if the elves or faeries or whoever they are making the light, try to make contact through a gateway they would usually use, but cannot get through, then that will be a lantern needing their light. So, they now know where to use their magic."

Molly, sitting cross-legged on the settee – like someone in a meditating position – was stunned by how simple Tom's solution seemed to be. But was it?

"This is a great answer to the problem Tom. A brilliant answer. But I suppose some lights might not be working because they have another problem, not the lack of sunlight."

Just then, Molly's mum came into the living room and said;

"Well, Molly Stevens, it is now almost ten o'clock and you have still not had any breakfast. Its high time you had some. You are very welcome to stay and have some breakfast with Molly, Tom."

"Thank you, Mrs Stevens, but I had my breakfast at about eight o'clock. I think I should be going back home anyway."

As soon as he'd said it, Tom got up from the armchair and walked towards the living room door. He turned to look at Molly.

"I'll think hard about that Molly and see if I can find an answer."

"So will I Tom and...thank you so much for coming over this morning."

Chapter Twenty

Unicorn raced through the Great Wood. He was seeking one of the most elusive figures in The Land of Faerie.

A Unicorn's senses are very finely tuned and at this time, Unicorn was relying on all of them to be working at 100 percent.

As he ran, he scanned the wood up and down, left, and right, to find any sign of who he was looking for.

He had covered a great distance across the Wood without any success. He stopped and rested for a short time. Just then, a very small bird – which was like our wren – landed on his shoulder. Unicorn turned his head to look at the small bird.

"And what do you want Mr Wrangling?"

"Good day, Sir Unicorn. If I am not mistaken, I think you seek 'The Light Maker'?"

"You are not mistaken Mr Wrangling. Do you know where I can find them?"

"I do, Sir Unicorn and The Light Maker has sent me to guide you."

Unicorn nodded and at that signal the small bird flew into the air and settled on the branch of a tree. Once Unicorn was looking in the right direction Mr Wrangling flew off, more-or-less in an easterly direction.

Unicorn followed the small bird flying in-and-out of the trees, just twenty metres above the ground. They had both been travelling for some minutes and then Mr Wrangling suddenly stopped, hovering as best he could, a few feet from the ground.

Unicorn stopped also and looked around. He was in a part of The Wood he had rarely visited and was alert to the possibility of strange creatures which might be dangerous. He did not sense any, but equally, he could not see or sense The Light Maker. He stood, very still.

Then, the bushes and shrubs only ten metres in front of him began to move and shake.

Gradually, a creature started to emerge from the undergrowth.

At first, Unicorn thought it was a fish. It had a head like a fish.

But how can that be? he thought to himself, We are a very long way from water.

But as the creature continued to come out from the bushes and shrubs it was clear it wasn't a fish at all. It had a long body and walked on several legs. In our human world, it was most like a lizard. However, it's skin was not damp, and it didn't flick its tongue in and out as lizards often do in our world. In fact, its skin was furry, and it had very kind eyes – not at all like the cold eyes of lizards and other reptiles in our world today.

"Good day Sir Unicorn. I have been expecting you."

Unicorn was taken by surprise by this but tried not to show it.

"Good day to you sir...? I am sorry but I do not know your name."

The creature smiled. It was a very friendly smile.

"I am Aonani, Mistress of the Light, or who you and others call The Light Maker."

Unicorn dropped onto his knees and bowed his head. He had only ever heard of "Aonani" in stories told to him many centuries ago, when he was a young Unicorn. She was a mystical and mythical creature with great powers, to be feared and revered as one might do to a god.

Aonani smiled. It was another very warm and friendly smile.

"I sense you have been told that I am to be feared, Sir Unicorn. Please do stand to your normal height. You have nothing to fear from me."

Unicorn stood up but he kept his head slightly bowed and did not look directly at The Light Maker. She was used to this reaction from other creatures in the Wood whenever they encountered her – though this was not very often as she was a very secretive creature. In fact, she had not seen another creature from the Wood for more than 200 years, except for the Wrangling who had become a close companion, as his parents, their parents, and grandparents, had been. Unicorn then said, as if to the ground in front of him;

"I sense you know already, Mistress of the Light, that the Elves need help to maintain connections with the human world."

"I believe that the problem is with light, Sir Unicorn. But I do not understand how I am expected to help with this. You must explain." Unicorn had known as he set out on his quest to find The Light Maker that he would have to explain.

"Well, my Mistress of the Light, it is complicated, but I will try to make it as simple as I can." He then proceeded to describe the events that led him to be with her today.

Aonani was clearly in thoughtful mood, staring at the heavens, and not moving at all. Then, after a short time, she suddenly jumped into the air. Unicorn could not help but look up at what was happening.

"I now understand the problem my very good friends, the elves and faeries, have, Sir Unicorn. However, I cannot help them with this problem."

Unicorn was distressed to hear these words. Who else could possibly help them? Aonani could see his distress at what she had said.

"I am sorry to cause you so much distress Sir Unicorn, but what I should have said is that I cannot help with this problem on my own. I will need to call on my "Sisters of the Light."

Sir Unicorn stared in disbelief at Aonani. He had always been told there was but one Light Maker. Could it be there were others?

"Yes, Sir Unicorn, there are others of us." Aonani had read his thoughts. "But it will take me some time to contact them, explain the problem, and get them involved. It will not be easy. We are, as you know, a secretive family."

Unicorn had already breathed several sighs of relief and was now feeling much more positive. However, he still wondered how many Sisters of the Light there were. Once again, Aonani could read his thoughts.

"I have 12 sisters, Sir Unicorn. They each have five or six children. We do not contact each other very often. The last time I remember speaking or 'mind-melding' with any of them is at least one hundred years ago. So, they might have many more offspring by now. And those offspring might have children of their own".

Arithmetic had never been a strong point for Unicorn but he suspected there could be at least 70 or maybe more relatives of Aonani.

"And, might I ask, Mistress of the Light, do each of the offspring have the ability to 'make light' from their early days?"

Aonani smiled, and said, "It is something that we are born to do, Sir Unicorn. However, not everyone does it as well as another immediately they leave their mother. Some must practice a little. Some have to practice a lot." Aonani smiled but she noticed that Unicorn was not smiling. He looked perturbed.

"I sense, Sir Unicorn, you believe the problem that the elves have is larger than my Sisters and I can manage."

"The fact is, my Mistress, I do not know."

Now it was the turn of Aonani to look perplexed. She had thought that Unicorn knew the scale of the problem and not just what it was. Unicorn continued.

"I am sorry, Mistress of the Light, but neither I nor anyone in our world knows exactly the scale of the problem but I have a friend in the Other World who is seeking an answer to that question. Aonani stared at Unicorn, then said;

"I am afraid, Sir Unicorn, that it is pointless me trying to contact my sisters until I can tell them the whole story. They will need to judge how they might help and then decide if they will try. I suggest you return to me here once you have the whole story." At that, she turned and called to Mr Wrangling. It was a strange language that she used, and one Unicorn had not heard before. He guessed, however, that Aonani was asking Mr Wrangling to help him find this place again when he was looking for her.

"Thank you, Mistress of the Light. I will proceed with all speed to find the answers you need and return here to ask again for your help."

Aonani bowed to him and then disappeared into the bushes almost in the blink of an eye.

Unicorn turned on his heels and went back to that part of the Great Wood where he knew he had the best chance of contacting Molly through her dreams.

Chapter Twenty-One

Half-way back to his chosen place for meeting with Molly, Unicorn felt – as he had once before – a very strong pull from Molly to talk with him. So, he suddenly disappeared from sight and within an instant he was where he wanted to be. It was the place where Molly usually appeared in The Wood.

He stood, waiting, and as usual took the chance to graze on the wonderfully luscious green grass which grew there. The pull from Molly remained strong. If anything, it was becoming stronger. Then he heard her calling his name.

She was not far away but he couldn't see her. He peered into the distance and looked all around. Still no sign of her. She called again, and again, and then he realised she was in the air. He looked at a distant, very large, silver birch tree. It was certainly extremely old.

There in some of its top branches was Molly. Unicorn had no idea what she was doing there and, judging by her calls to him, neither had she. He ran to the foot of the tree, looked-up, and called back to her.

"I am here Molly. What are you doing in the tree?"

Molly looked down as she clung, very firmly, onto a sturdy branch near her.

"I do not know Unicorn. And more importantly I do not know how to get down from here."

Unicorn smiled, inwardly, to himself.

"The quickest way is to jump, Molly."

Molly looked at him with a horrified expression. "It must be one hundred metres to the ground Unicorn. I would certainly break legs or arms or even die if I tried that."

"It isn't that high Molly, but I do agree it is quite high. But you need not fear. I will ensure you land softly on the ground."

"And how will you do that Unicorn?"

"Well, first you must remember you are in a dream. Many things are possible in your dreams. But second, I can make sure that you land safely. Remember, Unicorns have magical powers."

Molly thought for a while. Then, she counted.

"One, two, three," and jumped down directly towards Unicorn. However, on her way down through the branches her skirt snagged on a small branch. She was pulled to a stop. It was not long before her skirt ripped and she was free of the branch and she fell to the ground, landing safely on both feet. She had no idea whether this was a result of Unicorn's magic or the fact she was in a dream. Either way, she was a happy young girl.

"Well, Molly, it is good to see you again. And I think you want to speak with me? Certainly, I would like to speak with you."

Molly looked down at her torn skirt and tried to move it so it didn't gape so much.

"Oh heck. My mum will go wild when she sees this. It is my favourite skirt, and it is quite new. What can I do Unicorn?"

Unicorn smiled a warm smile looking down at the young girl.

"There is no need to do anything, Molly. Remember, you are in a dream, so it isn't torn or damaged at all in your real world. However, I am sure we can make it good if it is troubling you so much." And at that moment, the skirt was like new again.

Molly looked down, felt the skirt all around and, sure enough, it was just like the day it was bought.

"But how did you do that Unicorn?" Unicorn smiled and simply said, "I have told you before that we have some special powers. Anyway, what was it you wanted to talk with me about?"

Molly's head seemed to be buzzing but then she remembered that it was about the lanterns and her conversation with Tom.

"Well, you remember I am sure that we have a problem with how to identify the lights which need light to make them work?" Unicorn nodded.

"You have also said that you think creatures here in The Land of Faerie might be able to provide light for them." Unicorn nodded again. Molly took a deep breath. "Well, the only solution for those creatures knowing which lanterns need their light that we can think of is if the elves and faeries here in The Land of Faerie try to contact them and if they can't, then their gateways probably have a problem with getting light."

Unicorn didn't respond at all for some time. He simply stood, very still, and stared into the distance across The Wood and beyond where Molly was standing. Molly wondered what he was doing and, indeed, whether he had heard what she had said. Or could it be that he didn't understand what she had said? Just at that moment, Unicorn looked down at her and said, simply, "This is a great idea Molly, and we think it can work." Molly was taken by surprise with Unicorn using "we". He never used the plural unless he was talking on behalf of several folk. 'But,' she said to herself, 'there is no one here but him and me.' Molly was about to ask him what he meant by "we" when Unicorn anticipated her question.

"Ah, Molly. I see you wonder to whom I am referring when I say 'we'."

"Well, it had crossed my mind, Unicorn."

"You noticed, I believe, that I was very still and very quiet for a little time just now." Molly nodded. "Well, I was 'speaking' with the main creature, as you call them, who can provide light. I was asking whether your plan would be workable for them. And the Mistress of the Light answered, 'yes'." Molly smiled, probably the widest smile Unicorn had ever seen on her face. Then Molly began to jump up and down and wave her arms in the air – a sure sign she was pleased and excited. She was about to ask Unicorn when they might start this way of working when she started to leave her dream. There was nothing Unicorn could do to stop this process.

When Molly had almost disappeared, Unicorn set-off across The Great Wood to try and find The Light Maker.

Chapter Twenty-Two

Molly woke in a sweat, as if she had been in a nightmare. Of course, it was anything but a nightmare. She could remember everything from the dream.

She raced downstairs, said a very brief, "Hello Mum. Have to see Tom urgently," as she went out the front door.

She knocked on the front door of Tom's house and heard his dad shout, "It's Molly Tom. I suspect for you." Tom came to the door and he and Molly went into the garden.

"You look very pale, Molly. Is everything OK?"

"Yes, yes. I am fine. In fact, I feel very good indeed. You see, Unicorn has spoken....well, more, made contact with, The Light Maker, and we agreed that if the elves try to contact the normal lantern that they use to speak with humans, and cannot get through, then that is a lantern which probably needs light in order to function. And they can then provide light to that lantern. Isn't it brilliant Tom?"

Tom wasn't looking particularly pleased. He had his face screwed-up in a quizzical way, as if he was asking himself a question to which he didn't know the answer. Molly looked at him and began to laugh at the expression on his face.

"So, what are you laughing at Molly Stevens?" he said, somewhat irritated.

"I'm looking at your funny face. What are you thinking about?"

"Well, Miss know-it-all, for one thing I'm wondering just how these creatures can make light. And, for another, how they expect to send it to the lights in our world."

Molly knew Tom would ask these questions at some point. He was a very clever young man. "I don't know the answer to either of those questions, Mr Clever-Clogs, and I don't care how they do it. Unicorn says they can do it and that is good enough for me." Tom's shoulders slumped. He knew it was no good arguing with Molly when she was in this kind of mood, and especially where the Unicorn, elves and faeries were concerned.

"Anyway, what's more important is that we go to the lantern in my garden and see if the elves can get through to speak to me, er...I mean...us. Are you going to come?"

Tom got up from the grass and said, "You bet I'm coming." And at that, Tom went into his house and told his mum where he was going, then he and Molly both ran to Molly's house. When they got there, Molly was about to go straight into the garden but on the way through the kitchen her mum asked her what she was going to do. Molly explained she was going to switch-on the lanterns and wait to see if the elves could get through to speak to her.

"OK Molly but don't be too long. We are having an early lunch today because your aunty is coming to see us this afternoon so we will have an early tea."

"OK Mum. Can Tom stay for lunch?" Molly's mum said he could, but that he might need to telephone his Mum to let her know. Tom went into the hallway for a little privacy and called his mum on his mobile.

"Everything is fine with my mum, Mrs Stevens. Thank you for asking me to have lunch with you." Molly's mum smiled and said,

"OK. Now off you both go into the garden. I've got a lot of work to do in here." Neither Molly nor Tom needed asking twice and immediately ran outside and into the garden.

Molly switched on the light which glowed with just the faintest of light.

"So, what do we do now then Moll?" Molly glared at Tom.

"Don't call me that you, you…. oh, never mind. Anyway, I guess we just wait to see if the elves try to get through."

"Isn't there a time when you would normally talk to them? Molly thought about it for a little while, then said that there was a time and day. It was normally on Saturdays around three o'clock. Tom looked at his watch.

"Well, today is Saturday but it is only eleven-thirty in the morning."

"Oh heck. I bet that three o'clock today is when my auntie will be here. Mum certainly won't like me being out here waiting to hear from the elves when she is here. Anyway, we'll probably be having an early tea at that time."

Molly slumped down onto the garden Tomch near to the lantern. Tom sat down beside her. They sat in silence and only moving occasionally to look up at the lantern. It didn't change. After a while, Tom broke the silence.

"Why don't you try and contact the Unicorn, Molly? Maybe, when some of the elves talk with their human friends, they can ask them to tell others to be sure to have their lights on at the time they would normally speak together? It's what I have heard my dad call 'the bush telegraph' which, I think, means passing information by word of mouth. What do you think Moll...sorry, I mean Molly?"

At first Molly didn't respond or move then, suddenly, she jumped up off the seat and shouted, "Yes, and I could also ask him to tell 'my elves' to contact me before three o'clock."

"Go for it Molly."

Chapter Twenty-Three

Unicorn was very close to where he last met The Light Maker. He looked around to see if he could see Mr Wrangling who might guide him to the exact place where she was. Mr Wrangling was nowhere to be seen. Unicorn stood and tried to use his own powers to discover where The Light Maker might be. He had stood for only a few seconds and then he began to hear movement in the undergrowth of bushes and other flowers.

"Ah, Sir Unicorn. I see it is you who calls me. You have news, perhaps, of what I hear is called the Great Quest?"

"I do Mistress of the Light."

"Then please proceed with your news."

"The idea of the human is that if elves who normally contact their human friends try to do so and cannot make contact, it probably means the gateway needs light to work. Then, those elves must be sure to tell you and your sisters so you can send your light to those gateways."

The Light Maker stood (or maybe sat, it was hard to tell) and did not move for a long time – at least as time passes in the World of Faerie. Then she suddenly said, "This can work but, in my view, we will need the help of The Messengers who were sent from The Gathering to give the message spoken by elven Queen Carolina to all elves and all other creatures in The Wood about The Great Quest, as she named it. Making sure those Messengers know this is, I believe, a task for you Sir Unicorn."

Unicorn had not expected such a task to be given to him, but his shoulders were broad, and he was more than willing to shoulder the burden.

"I will make sure all the Messengers are given their task and the reason for it, Mistress of the Light, but where should they be told to find you and your sisters so they can pass the information to you?"

"They should be told to come to The Ancient White Oak. Everyone in The Great Wood knows where that is. We will be there to receive their news, Sir Unicorn"

Unicorn bowed to The Light Maker, and no sooner had he done that, than she disappeared back into the bushes.

Unicorn began to think how he could complete the task he had in the shortest time. He decided he needed the help of the Prince and Princesses, and maybe even the elven Queen herself. So, he decided to try and connect with them, mind-to-mind. It was not long before Princess Josephina responded. Then Esmeralda, followed by Prince Charlelot and finally by Queen Carolina herself.

Unicorn had not rehearsed what he needed to say but he tried to choose his 'words' carefully.

'My dear Queen, Princesses, and Prince. I have contacted the human called Molly and now spoken with The Light Maker. The only solution we have to The Great Quest is to make sure that all the elves who regularly speak with their human friends report to The Light Maker and her Sister Light Makers about whether they have been able to make contact.' He paused in his thoughts, briefly, and then continued, 'where they haven't been able to make contact is where The Light Maker, and her sisters, will focus their efforts to bring light to the lanterns.' He paused again, this time to see if those his mind was connected to had any questions. They didn't seem to have. So, he continued to his final part of the message. 'The Light Maker believes that it will be best if the information is bought to them by The Messengers. They should go to The Ancient White Oak and there they will be able to pass on their messages.' Once again there was a pause but then he received thoughts from Princess Esmeralda.

'This seems like a good way forward, but we will need to get this plan to all the Messengers.

'And,' Princess Josephina said, 'The Messengers and all others must get the message to every elf who has contact with humans.'

'I believe we can ensure that every one of our kinsfolk in our own Woods gets the message. We should each call Prince or Princess meetings. All elves will be sure to come to those.' These were the thoughts of Queen Carolina. So far, Prince Charlelot had not contributed to the conversation. Everyone waited but he was silent. Queen Carolina's thoughts were to the point.

'You agree with the plan, Prince Charleot?' There was silence but then his thoughts came through clearly.

'I will do what is agreed.'

'Good,' said the Queen, 'Then we set to our tasks immediately. Sir Unicorn, you have worked hard and tirelessly to get us to this important stage in The Great Quest. Now it is our turn and that of The Messengers. You should rest. There may be more for you to do in the future but for now go with our good wishes.'

'Thank you, dear Queen.'

At that the 'mind-meld' ended and the next stage of the Great Quest began.

Chapter Twenty-Four

Although he was grateful for the Queen's instruction to rest, Unicorn knew he had one task still to do. He had to be sure that the elves with whom Molly spoke through her lantern – Maple Leaf, Iris Flower, Mayfly and Clematis – knew they needed to try to get through to her before mid-afternoon human time. And, if they couldn't, then the Messengers needed to get that message the Light Maker.

Unicorn believed he knew exactly where Maple Leaf and Mafly lived. For one thing, all the elves in Western Wood had names of flowers or trees or parts of trees or flowers. At first, he thought he must gallop as fast as he could through The Great Wood to Western Wood. He set-off but then stopped sharply in his tracks. It would be much faster to pass on the message through mind-melding with their Princess – Princess Josephina. So began to think powerfully and strongly of Josephina, using his special powers to ensure she knew his attempt to contact her was urgent.

'Sir Unicorn. I had not expected to hear from you for a long time', she 'said'. 'I sense it is something urgent you want from me.'

Unicorn then explained as briefly as he could what he needed to be done and asked if she could make it happen.

'I know Mayfly very well, but I must admit I do not believe I have met Maple Leaf, Iris Flower or Clematis. No matter. I will ensure Mayfly gets the message as soon as we have finished. So, is that all you need of me?' Unicorn said it was and with that the mind-meld was ended.

Unicorn felt he must somehow tell Molly what was happening, but he was almost completely exhausted and knew he needed to rest. 'In any event', he said to himself, 'I feel sure Molly will try to contact me if her lantern starts to work using light from the Light Maker. So, he trotted a short distance to a very large tree and lay down beside it to sleep. He went to sleep almost immediately.

Chapter Twenty-Five

Molly kept looking at the clock in the dining room as she helped her Mum lay the table for a very grand afternoon tea. Tom had left a short time earlier, after Molly's mum had called her to come and help in the dining room. Molly was so very, very eager to get into the garden to see if the lantern might be working. She was not confident at all but nevertheless hoped beyond hope that it would be.

It was almost 2:30 before she had finished helping her Mum, and she knew her aunty was due to arrive at three o'clock. Her mum looked at her and started laughing.

"OK young lady I know you want to get to your lantern so off you go. I'll call you when your aunty arrives, and I expect you to come and meet her straightaway. Do I make myself clear?"

"Yes Mum," Molly said, as she was leaving the dining room through the patio doors to go into the garden.

She got to the lantern, held her breath, and switched it on. It gave just a pale, faint glow. Molly knew it wasn't working properly. Once again, as before when Tom had been with her, she slumped down onto the garden seat near the lantern. She stared down at the ground. She felt like crying. All those efforts to try and fix the lanterns caused by the effects of global dimming and global warming. She sat in complete silence. Soon, she knew, she would get the call from her mum, and she would have to go to see her aunty straightaway.

Then she heard a noise, a little like a crackling sound. She couldn't tell where it was coming from. It was very faint and sounded to be from far away. She looked around but couldn't see anything. Then she looked at the lantern. It was glowing quite brightly and getting brighter by the minute. She jumped off the seat and went to look into the lantern. And there she was. It was Mayfly.

Just then, Molly's mum called her to come inside as her aunty was getting out of her car.

"Mum, just five minutes. Pleeeeeese? Can I have just five minutes?" Her mum scowled. You can have three minutes and I'll be timing."

Molly looked back into the lantern.

"Hello Mayfly. You are back. How wonderful it is to see you."

"And for me to see you, Molly."

Molly then heard her Mum's voice.

"Molleeeeeeeee!"

THE END